# WHAT THE HEART WANTS

Book Cover by Delaney Leffler

*To the ones who believed in me from the very start.*

# Playlist

Music has always been a very important part of my writing process. Below are the songs I listened to almost exclusively while writing. These songs evoke the essence of these characters in my mind and I hope it helps you feel even more connected to them.

What Baking Can Do - Waitress Original Broadway Cast

Dreams - Fleetwood Mac

Go Your Own Way - Fleetwood Mac

Silver Springs - Fleetwood Mac

Can't Fight This Feeling - Glee Cast cover

Body And Mind - girl in red

chemtrails - Lizzy McAlpine

Isimo - Bleachers

What the Heart Wants - Collin Raye

Little Wonders - Rob Thomas

Breaking Down - Florence + The Machine

Between The Lines - Sara Bareilles

La Vie En Rose - Emily Watts

Hold My Heart - Sara Bareilles

how well do you know your feelings - Alice Merton
I Don't Care - Fall Out Boy
Ruin The Friendship - Taylor Swift
Opalite - Taylor Swift
Gold Rush Kid - George Ezra
Eyes On You (Live From the Hollywood Bowl) - Sara Bareilles
merry christmas, i miss you - Alex Crichton
Audrey Hepburn - Maisie Peters
So Easy (To Fall in Love) - Olivia Dean
I Wanna Get Better - Bleachers
Buckle - Florence + The Machine
Salt Then Sour Then Sweet - Sara Bareilles ft. Brandi Carlile
Wish That You Were Here - Florence + The Machine
Guilty as Sin? - Taylor Swift

# Chapter One

## Thea

I can feel my heartbeat in my ears. My throat feels like it's closing up, but I try not to gasp for air. I run my fingers over the woven fabric of my seatbelt, trying to ground myself.

It only takes a second for your life to be changed forever.

Unfortunately for me, my life was changed on the evening of January thirteenth when my mom and I were involved in a head-on collision.

*It was a typical January day in Seattle, cold and dreary. It was one of my last days off from college before a new semester began. It was also one of the rare days where Mom wasn't even on-call as a practicing neurosurgeon. We spent the entire day shopping and only stopped when we got hungry. The snow started falling while we were enjoying our dinner, blanketing the city in soft, pure flakes. It was a wet kind of snow that night, the kind you wish for as a kid. The kind that makes for great snowmen and snowball fights. We were on the way home, arguing over the radio volume when I noticed a pair of headlights heading in the wrong direction, the car sliding through a stop sign on the slushy road...*

"Thea," my aunt says, pulling me out of the memory.

"What?" I ask. I shake my head to banish the ghostly memories away. They haunt me more than I'd like to admit.

"I asked if you were hungry. The diner is just a little ways up." She gestures out the windshield at the road in front of us.

"Oh. No, I'm okay." I shift awkwardly in the passenger seat, trying to get comfortable. I've spent all day cooped up on planes and now I am crammed in Aunt Beth's car.

Beth nods silently and keeps driving. The only sounds in the car are the hum of the air conditioner blasting and the Fleetwood Mac song coming from the stereo. I recognize it immediately as it was one of my mother's favorite songs. I like to think that it's her way of smiling down on me and approving of this cross-country move to Driftbay, South Carolina.

I brush a strand of my blonde hair out of my face as tears well in my eyes. I blink them away as I stare out the window, willing my mind to think of something else, anything else. I don't want to break down here. Not here, not in front of Aunt Beth. I don't want to make her cry as well. She worries about me enough as it is.

I fiddle with the delicate chain around my neck; a necklace given to me by my mom for my high school graduation — a simple peridot stone, my birthstone, on a thin gold chain. She thought it matched my eyes. She'd also said it was sophisticated and elegant and as a young woman on the verge of adulthood, that's what I should portray.

Sophistication and elegance. Those are not the words I would use to describe myself. I am messy and clumsy, a catastrophe compared to my mother.

By eighteen, she had her life figured out. She knew what she wanted and she went after it. She never fully put down roots until she had me. She always used to say that I grounded her, in more ways than one. Part of me always wondered if she ever resented me for that.

At twenty, I still don't know what I want to do with my life — a far cry from my mother's preparedness in her own. I have spent the last six months trying to rebuild my life. I left college, unable to continue on with the amount of grief that now consumes me. I lost nearly all of the new friends I'd made after that. Sure, they checked in at the beginning, but slowly and surely the texts and calls stopped coming. My friends from high school are spread out all across the country and sent their condolences, but the only one that really stood by me has been my best friend, Ireland.

Everyone worries about you in the beginning but it's the middle that could use some work.

It was within those six months that I decided to move across the country and live with my mom's sister, my aunt Beth Ann, in the quiet, coastal town of Driftbay. She has welcomed me with open arms, having no spouse or children of her own. In a matter of weeks, I cleaned out our apartment in Seattle and packed up my life. I need a fresh start and Beth's beachside escape seems like the perfect place to get it.

Miles of coast pass before me, peaceful and serene. This is exactly what someone like me needs — a quiet, gentle place to unpack the tumultuous storm of grief rumbling within. Seattle took so much from me; it chewed me up and spit me back out in nothing flat. Continuing college just feels like too big a mountain to climb at the moment, so my plan for the upcoming future...well, to be honest, I don't really have one. When you go from an honors student to flunking out, you have to take stock of the damage you've created and pump the brakes.

I just want to live. Or at least find a reason to again. Sometimes I feel guilty for making it out alive when my mother didn't. She was a world-renowned surgeon, a gift to others, a lifesaver, and I'm just...me.

Beth hits the turn signal and makes a left off the freeway. I focus my breathing on matching the chirp of her turn signal — in and out. We drive a little ways further and she makes another left before pulling off the road onto a gravel driveway. She drives up to her house, a quaint, white cottage at the edge of the beach. Her backyard is miles of sandy shoreline. The cottage is small, but from the few times I've been inside it, it's plenty big enough for the two of us.

She shuts the engine off and we sit in silence for a few moments before she turns to me, sliding her sunglasses on top of her head through her dark brown hair. There's gray in the front strands, cruel evidence of time passing.

"Welcome back," she says, her light blue eyes sparkling. She smiles at me and I offer a weak one back. "It's not much, but it's home," she adds as she opens her car door.

The cottage and porch are a weathered white, with obvious patches of paint chipping and peeling on the porch. Weeds have taken over the narrow flower bed around the edge of the steps; Aunt Beth never could be bothered to get her hands in the dirt.

"It's perfect," I say as I open my door, hopping out to stretch my legs. It may look a little rough around the edges, but to me, it's welcoming and cozy. The kind of place that's lived in. I take a deep breath in, letting the salty air fill and stretch my lungs. I feel the anxiety dissolve as I take another deep breath. It feels nice to be out of the car and moving around.

I follow Aunt Beth to the back of her small sedan and help retrieve the last of my belongings. She lugs my bigger suitcase around the cottage and up the porch steps. As she unlocks the back door, I grab my duffle bag and shut the trunk. Memories of the past play out in front of me as I follow in her steps to the back porch.

*"Do you ever pull your weeds?" Mom asks as she carries a bag to the porch, eyeing the overgrown vegetation around the base.*

*Aunt Beth smiles at us from the top step. "I don't really have time for that," she says.*

*"Of course not," Mom laughs. "I forgot you live at the diner." She trudges up the steps of the porch.*

*"Like how you live at the hospital?" Beth retorts.*

*"It's nice to see you, too," Mom says before she and Aunt Beth wrap each other in a bear hug. Then they both turn to me and open their arms wide.*

"You coming?" Beth calls over her shoulder and the memory vanishes.

I follow after her and the screen door slams behind me as we walk into the house.

Beth tosses her keys into a bowl on the small, thin wooden table in the entryway before she points to her right. "The kitchen is over here."

I trip over the navy rug in front of the door and regain my footing, awkwardly shuffling my duffle bag.

"I remember," I say, finding my voice again. I feel a timid smile creep along my face. I glance in its direction. The late-afternoon sunlight is streaming in through the sheer white curtains hanging above the sink. A small wooden table and four green-upholstered chairs sit in the corner.

"Right." Beth smiles again. "Of course."

I can tell she is a bit anxious, as well. I think back to the times Mom and I visited her when I was a kid. We didn't get out here that often. My mother barely had time to raise a child — by herself, I might add — let alone take a vacation across the country. She was a workaholic, in simplest terms. Aunt Beth is the same in her own way. She claims she is a free spirit and doesn't want to be tied down by a traditional nine-to-five. So of course, she also chose a job with almost no days off. The diner could survive without her but I know her well enough to know that she can't stand to be away from her routine and regulars for more than a couple of days.

She leads me past the living room, another room full of white. There's a flatscreen television hanging above the fireplace mantle, along with built-in bookshelves full of all sorts of novels. A fluffy, white couch sits in the center of the room and I see another door in the corner, leading to Beth's bedroom.

We head down a small hallway, towards the back of the house to the guest bedroom. It's a decent enough space — big windows overlooking the coast framed by sheer, white curtains, and stark white walls. A lot of white. I can do anything I want with it, she tells me.

I can't help but think that Driftbay is the bedroom in the floor plan of my life — fresh and full of possibilities.

A queen-size bed sits in the middle of the room and looks like the most inviting thing after my long day of travel — two connecting flights and an hour drive back to the cottage. A dresser and a vanity line two of the walls. Boxes scatter the floor, full of my belongings, but a few stacked on top are open.

"I wasn't going through your things," Beth begins quickly, seeing me eye the boxes. "I just wanted to have the bed already made up for you. Figured you could use a good night's rest after the day you've had."

"Thank you." The duffle bag I'm holding hits the floor with a soft thud. "I appreciate it more than you know."

I walk towards the dresser in the corner of the room and notice a framed photograph on top of it. I pick it up to look at it closer — it's Mom, Beth, and me on the beach from our last trip together. A younger version of myself smiles back at me through the glass. I must have been in eighth grade or maybe a freshman in high school during that trip. I remember that trip fondly, spending the week lazily laying on the beach.

My heart swells at the memory and I set the frame down before the tears can come. You never know the last time is the last time.

"Do you want help unpacking?" Beth asks. "I'm not going to the diner tonight or tomorrow, so I can help with whatever you need."

"I'd really like a shower first, if I'm honest," I say. I feel gross from the airports and being around so many strangers.

She nods. "Towels and washcloths are in the closet in the bathroom, help yourself." She sticks her hands in the pockets of her jean shorts. "I'll leave you to it."

She turns to leave and it hits me just how vastly different my mom and aunt are. Mom was short, but like Shakespeare said, "though she be little, she be fierce." You didn't want to challenge Caroline Calloway. She cursed like a sailor when she was mad, something that secretly always made me giggle. She was brilliant; she saved lives on the daily. Her eyes were the brightest green I'd ever seen, the kind that caught golden flecks of sunlight. She kept her reddish, caramel brown hair short, hitting just in line with her chin. She liked to garden in her limited spare time. Mom was loud, expressive, and ferocious; a force to be reckoned with.

Aunt Beth, on the other hand, is more guarded than her counterpart. She's soft where my mother was rough. Beth has the prettiest light blue eyes — the kind of blue that burns cold, sharp as ice. It's hard to look her in the eyes for long, especially when she's angry — something she uses to her advantage. Her hair falls past her shoulders and is a dark, chocolate brown. She's taller than me and a half a foot taller than Mom. While Mom was poised and polished, Aunt Beth is less put together. She's quiet, inquisitive, and pensive. She thinks before she speaks.

Beth is the calm and my mother was the storm.

I pick up my duffle bag and pull out a sweatshirt and leggings before I head down the hallway. A hot and steamy shower is calling my name.

A delicate rose wallpaper covers every inch of the wall space in the tiny bathroom. There's a white porcelain vanity to my left. I catch a glimpse of my reflection in the mirror of the medicine cabinet above the sink and sigh. Whether it's the grief that permanently resides in my face, or the day of travel, or both, I look like death warmed over. My green eyes, so similar to my mother's, lack their usual sparkle. I think my spark died with her.

I rub my face and then pull my hair tie out, letting my hair fall down my shoulders before I turn the water on. I let it warm up a bit before I strip my clothes off and toss them into a pile on the floor and climb in.

I wake up the next morning, faced with my new normal. I stare at the ceiling fan above me, watching as the blades lazily make their laps. It takes a moment to orient myself, to realize that after months of daydreaming about it, I am finally in Driftbay. Early-morning sunlight spills through the sheer curtains onto the hardwood floor. I get out of bed and stretch before going to the windows and opening them. The floor is cold beneath my feet. It's still cool outside for mid-June. I take a deep breath in and pause for a moment, letting the salty air fill my lungs. The crashing waves conduct a calming melody, and I time my breathing with them. Seattle was a loud, upbeat tune — one I'm glad to no longer be hearing.

I stare at the boxes for a bit, knowing I need to unpack, before I decide to go in search of Aunt Beth. I find her outside on the back porch, curled up in one of the navy Adirondack chairs with a cup of coffee and a book, still in her pajamas. She startles briefly at my presence before closing her book, tossing her bookmark in haphazardly. I settle into the chair beside her.

"Morning," she says.

"Morning," I echo back. My voice lacks the cheerfulness hers does.

"Sleep okay?" she asks.

"Yeah." I pull my legs up to my chest. It wasn't a total lie; the serenity was going to take some getting used to. For quietness, it sure can be loud. I don't tell her about the nightmares I've been having; the images of the crash still haunting me in my slumber. "This is nice," I add, nodding my head toward the white sandy beach that makes up her backyard.

"There's a reason I never left after college." She gently sets her mug down on the white wicker table between us and smiles. I glance at the book in her lap; judging from the cover it looks like some kind of fantasy romance novel.

"Are you hungry?" she asks. "I was going to swing by the diner and grab breakfast for us and check in on them. My better cook is working this morning and I need to get groceries."

"Yes," I say, my stomach grumbling in agreement. I didn't eat dinner the night before so breakfast is a welcome treat.

"Bacon or sausage?" she asks as she stands.

"Uh, bacon," I reply, staring up at her.

She nods and then dashes inside to change out of her pajamas. She's changed and back out the door in an instant, leaving me alone with the comfort of the crashing waves. There's not many folks out on the beach this early. A few lone seagulls leisurely soar through the sky, talking to each other in their own language.

I'm not sure how long I spend outside consumed by my thoughts, but Beth is back before I know it. She jogs up the porch steps, plastic takeout bag in hand. I get out of the chair and follow her into the house, letting the screen door slam behind us.

"Were they surviving without you?" I ask as we walk into the kitchen.

Beth smiles as she sets the bag on the counter. She tucks a strand of hair behind her ear as she laughs. "Barely," she says before getting two plates from the cabinet. "I trust them, I do, but I just feel better if I'm there."

"You can go," I say. "I can unpack by myself, it's okay."

"Oh, I didn't mean it like that." Beth turns to me. "I want to be here with you. They just tend to do better if I'm there. It's fine, really."

I nod as she plates our breakfast. I sit down at the small table in the corner of the kitchen. Beth shuffles over to the refrigerator and pulls out a jug of orange juice before grabbing two glasses from the dish drainer in the sink. A huge grin stretches across her face as she presents breakfast to me — a smorgasbord of treats.

"Call it a homecoming breakfast," she says as she sets her own plate down and sinks down in the chair opposite of me.

My mouth waters at the aromas floating up to my nostrils. There's pancakes, hashbrown casserole, bacon, eggs, and biscuits. A true feast. We eat silently for a few moments before she starts telling me more about the diner, the staff members she wants me to meet, and about her day to day life in Driftbay. Our forks clang against the china as we talk.

"I want you to feel at home here," she says as she clears our plates from the table. "Truly. I know you're legally an adult now but I want this place to be your safe haven, somewhere you can always come back to."

I think it always has been. Sure, Mom and I didn't get out here a ton when I was younger, but some of my best memories from those days belong to the sand and sea. I would daydream about the next time we would get to see Aunt Beth and visit this piece of paradise before we'd even left it.

We spend the day unpacking my belongings and making her house feel like my home. By the end of the day, it's like I've lived here my entire life and Seattle is nothing but a distant memory. Aunt Beth plays some of her favorite records on her vinyl player in the living room and we end up dancing throughout the house as we unpack. It's nice getting to spend quality time with her again. Before Mom's celebration of life, I hadn't seen her since my high school graduation. We order pizza in and spend the night talking about Mom, having placed her urn in the center of the mantle in the living room — a focal point in the house and in our lives.

Beth plays one final record that evening — a Fleetwood Mac album she and Mom loved when they were teenagers. She pours herself a glass of wine and we dance and sing along to the melodies pounding through the house. We dance together well past sunset, for Mom and in honor of her. For a moment, I begin to feel lighter, like the weight of her death isn't crushing me.

Like maybe there's a reason to live.

# Chapter Two

## Thea

Aunt Beth is gone the next morning when I wake up. I trudge into the kitchen and spot a note on the table, her handwriting scribbled across it. She'd gone into the diner, so after a quick shower to help fully wake myself up, I decide to head there as well.

The diner is just a couple of blocks from the house, a short walk that I use to accustom myself to the neighborhood. It's quiet, filled with cottages like Beth's and tall-standing condos. A couple of kids are playing in a sprinkler in one front yard. They giggle and shriek with such childlike wonder it almost makes me jealous. I smile at them as I pass by, wishing I could revisit the days where bedtime was my biggest rival.

Beth Ann's Diner comes into view as I round the last corner. Like her cottage, it's quaint, but definitely not small. The outside of the diner is painted a lovely shade of blue, like her eyes, with white shutters on the windows. The parking lot is already full for nine in the morning but I've gathered that it's a pretty popular place on the coast. Tourists flock to it and of course, her regulars do, too.

A bell rings above my head as I push the door open and I'm blasted by a gush of air-conditioning. I glance around the diner; it's still the same from my memory, frozen in time. The walls are a light blue and decorated with lighthouse wallpaper, along with framed nautical posters and images. There's a jukebox in the corner and framed newspaper clippings line the wall behind the counter. It's homey and the kind of place you know you'll get quality service.

I spot Beth behind the counter and walk over to it, taking a seat at one of the bright blue barstools. Her uniform is simple — jeans, a white T-shirt, and black apron.

"Morning!" she says cheerfully as she sees me.

"Good morning," I offer in return, taking another glance around the place. There's a variety of customers in this morning. I see a tall and slender waitress at the corner booth, taking the order of a couple with two small children already clad in their swimsuits. The kids are climbing all over the booth, anxiously pointing out the window at the distant shore, ready for the beach day that awaits them. The waitress smiles as she talks with them and pops her bubblegum as she takes their order, her light-red hair gleaming in the morning light pouring through the window.

"Morning, Beth Ann," a gravelly voice calls out beside me.

I've never known anyone to call my aunt by her full name, even though it is the name of her restaurant.

"Morning, Charlie," Beth replies in a singsong voice. I can tell she's had her coffee this morning with how chipper she is. She slides a mug across the counter as Charlie swings a leg over the barstool beside me and sits down.

He's tall. He looks a bit taller than Beth. He's bald, and his face looks weathered. He has piercing dark blue eyes, and a muscular build, seemingly to be the type of man that works out every day.

"Right on time," I hear her add, tossing the words over her shoulder as she reaches across the kitchen window for a plate stacked high with crispy bacon and fluffy eggs.

I figure he must come here every day for her to already have his order ready.

I see Charlie smile behind the coffee mug that's at his lips as he takes a sip and his eyes settle on her backside. I cough awkwardly to remind him that he is not alone at the counter and is ogling my aunt.

Charlie sets his mug down and cocks his head in my direction. "Is this Thea?" he asks her.

I perk up, wondering what she has told him about me.

"It is." Beth smiles as she sets the plate down in front of him, steam rising from it in swirly streams. "Charlie, this is Thea. Thea, this is my friend and county sheriff, Charlie Gajewski."

Aunt Beth leans against the counter in front of us after making our introductions, crossing her arms on the cold metal surface. She's glowing this morning and exudes warmth as she watches us.

"It's a pleasure to meet you, Thea," Charlie says, extending his hand out to me. I shake it; he's got a firm grip.

"Nice to meet you, too." I offer a smile.

"How are you liking our little town?" he asks before stabbing his fork in his eggs.

"Good," I say, "it's a lot different than Seattle but I like it so far. It's calm."

He and Beth chuckle at my words. "You wouldn't say that if you were on the police force."

I find it hard to imagine a sleepy little town like Driftbay has that much action for the cops.

I offer another smile as Charlie and Beth become lost in a conversation of their own. He says something funny, I assume, because Aunt Beth throws her head back laughing like a little kid. Her laugh lines are more pronounced and her eyes glitter with delight. I've never seen her this animated. There's something going on between them, but I'm not sure what. I'll have to ask her about it later.

"Do you have any plans for the day?" Beth asks me as she looks in my direction, turning the conversation back to me.

"I think I'm going to go down to the beach for a little while," I say.

"I'm going later if you'd like to go with me." The waitress I noticed earlier joins us at the counter. "With Graham," she adds, nodding her head back towards the kitchen. "Unless you'd like to be alone." She tears a ticket out of her serving book and slides it across the kitchen window. She looks back at me through circular glasses and smacks her gum again before smiling. "Hi," she says as she extends her arm out. "I'm Raquel."

"Thea," I say as I shake her hand. "And actually, that seems fun. I'd love to go with you guys."

Beth smiles as she watches us. "Oh, I think you two would get along great!" She seems happy at the idea of us hanging out. "Raquel is my best waitress," she adds, as if that has any merit in our possible friendship.

Raquel's cheeks flame at my aunt's accolades, turning a fiery shade nearly the same color as her hair and her hazel eyes sparkle.

"Oh, stop," she says, playfully swatting Beth's arm. She looks back at me. "Shift change is at noon, so we could meet around twelve-fifteen? That would give me enough time to cash out and change clothes."

"Sure." I nod, my fingertips brushing the laminated menu on the counter in front of me. "That sounds great." I feel a smile spreading across my face.

"Are you hungry?" Raquel asks, nodding towards the menu as she pops her gum loudly.

"Yes, actually." I pick up the menu and glance at it for a moment before getting decision fatigue. I turn to Beth. "I'll just have what Charlie's having."

She nods and turns toward the kitchen window, hollering to get Graham's attention.

A tall, sandy-haired, blue-eyed boy appears in the kitchen window. Beth directs him to make another order of eggs and bacon and he listens intently. She turns back around and her eyes land on me.

"Oh! Graham!" she calls out.

Graham sticks his head back in the window.

"This is my niece, Thea." Beth gestures at me and I feel my cheeks start to burn as Graham's eyes dance over me. I can't help but notice the way his mouth curls into a smile when he's given me the once-over.

"Thea, this is Graham Gordon."

"Nice to meet you, Thea," he says as he grins, revealing a pearly white smile. He waves with the spatula in his hand before he disappears from view and I miss my chance to respond.

Raquel senses one of her tables needs her and is off again.

Beth and Charlie continue their conversation while I wait for my food. I turn around on my barstool to get a better look at the patrons in the diner. I'm lost in my thoughts for a few minutes before I hear the ding of the kitchen bell and turn back around as Beth grabs my breakfast. She slides it in front of me and suddenly, I'm famished. I bring a forkful to my mouth and inhale the aroma.

"These are so good," I mutter after I swallow the first bite, bringing a napkin to my lips.

"Told you Graham is my best cook," Beth says, nodding behind her to the kitchen window.

"Got any pie this morning, Beth Ann?" Charlie asks, folding his napkin in his large hands.

"You know I do," she laughs, putting a hand on her hip. "Blueberry, your favorite. Baked fresh this morning." Beth scurries off to the other end of the counter and then a plate of blueberry pie is placed in front of Charlie.

He takes a bite and lets his eyes close in delight. "Mmm," he hums, pointing his fork at the plate. "You never disappoint."

"You made that?" I ask her. She must have gotten up earlier than I thought.

"Mmhmm. I do all the baking for this place. It's a...form of solace for me."

There must be something in our genetics — baking is a form of solace for me, as well.

The three of us stay silent except for the scrapes of our forks as both Charlie and I clean our plates. The radio on Charlie's belt goes off, some code I don't know is announced. He throws a twenty down on the counter and tells Beth to keep the change on his way out the door.

Raquel comes back to the counter not long after he leaves.

"So," she begins as she leans against the countertop. "How are you liking Driftbay so far?"

That question seems to be the icebreaker on everyone's mind.

"Well," I start, "so far, so good. Like I told Charlie, it's a lot different than Seattle. But it's a good kind of different." I don't elaborate further or go into my tragic backstory.

"I've always wanted to visit Seattle," she says as she smacks her gum and plays with a strand of her hair absentmindedly.

"Do you travel?" I ask her.

Raquel shakes her head. "Not often. I tend to stick to Driftbay. I'm trying to save up money to go back to school." She smiles proudly. "But maybe we can visit together one day."

I smile politely and nod my head in agreement. Unbeknownst to her, I have no intention of ever visiting Seattle again.

We carry on our conversation for a little while longer, Beth joining in every now and then as she works the counter. It's not long until I decide to head back to the house to get ready for the beach.

I grab an old tote bag from the closet and toss in a beach towel and sunscreen. I retrieve my only swimsuit from the dresser and quickly change into it before sliding my shorts and T-shirt back over my body.

If I thought the diner was busy this morning, it's nothing compared to how it is when I come back to meet Raquel and Graham. There's a line out the door and wrapped around the porch. I get dirty looks from the waiting patrons as I squeeze past them to enter the restaurant. I'm blasted again by the air-conditioning and see Beth in her heyday with customers but don't bother her. I spot Raquel behind the counter at the register cashing out.

"Hey!" she says excitedly as she sees me. "Give me five minutes and I'll be ready." She offers a warm smile and it calms me.

I nod and go wait by the jukebox for her. I remember playing with it as a kid. I'm lost in thoughts of years past as another red-headed waitress comes on for shift change.

"Ready?" Raquel asks a few moments later, swinging her car keys around her index finger. Graham is following close behind her, carrying a surfboard.

"Hey, Thea." He nods to acknowledge me, shaking his hair out of his eyes.

"Hey."

The three of us walk out of the diner, Graham having to maneuver a bit more carefully around the crowd with his surfboard. Raquel digs around in her bag and pulls out a pair of oversized sunglasses. She's in more relaxed clothes now, jean shorts and an oversized band tee.

"Do you guys want to take my car or walk?" She looks at me and adds, "The beach is about four or five blocks from here."

"I'm good with whatever," Graham says, "though walking would probably be better with my board."

They look at me and I know the decision is mine. "We can walk," I say, feeling the tightness in my chest start at the thought of getting into a vehicle with people I barely know. "I don't mind."

"Okay!" Raquel takes off and Graham and I fall into line behind her. She seems like a happy-go-lucky kind of girl and part of me is jealous of that.

I used to be like that but life has a way of knocking you down sometimes.

"How was the rest of your shift?" I ask them as we walk.

"Not bad," Graham says. "I stayed busy. Helps the time go by quicker."

"Honestly, your aunt could afford to hire a few more people," Raquel says. "I love Beth, don't get me wrong, but she could use more help. She needs a general manager that's not her."

I nod. She *could* use more employees and give herself a bit of a break sometimes.

"I did make pretty good money in tips, though," Raquel adds. "So, at least my rent's paid."

"Nice. What about you, Graham?"

"Graham doesn't have to stress about rent." Raquel turns and grins at Graham.

"I still live at home," he says, shuffling his surfboard to his other arm. "I help my mom out, so it just makes sense."

"Have you always lived here?" I ask.

He nods again.

"The weather is gorgeous today," Raquel says, breaking up the conversation. "It's going to be a great beach day."

She's right. It's sunny and seventy-five, near perfect beach conditions.

We reach the beach and the two of them take off across the sand. I struggle to keep up with them, my feet sinking into the sand with each step. There are families scattered all along the coast, no doubt the beginning of peak season for Driftbay. We find a spot away from most of the crowd and start to set up camp. Graham secures the umbrella for us while Raquel strips off her clothes, revealing her black bikini.

I shrug off my shorts and T-shirt and reach for the sunscreen in my bag. I slather my arms and legs in it and am just starting on my neck and face when I hear Graham say, “Here.”

I open my eyes and look at him; his hand is outstretched and he’s waiting for the bottle. I hand it to him cautiously.

“Turn around, I’ll get your back.” He squirts some of the sunscreen into his hands as I turn around.

“Thanks,” I say timidly, feeling goosebumps prickle my skin as his hands work over my back.

His fingers linger a second too long on my skin before he hands me back the bottle of sunscreen.

“Good to go,” he says.

“Thanks,” I repeat, unsure of what to make of this interaction. I notice Raquel giving us a sly smile.

Graham picks up his surfboard and heads out into the water to take it for a spin. I grab my sunglasses from my bag and put them on as Raquel leans down to smooth out her beach towel. A neon green frisbee comes flying out of nowhere and hits me right in the neck.

I’m coughing and sputtering as the frisbee hits the ground at our feet.

“Oh my God, are you okay?” Raquel asks. “Who would even do that?” She looks around the beach to find the perpetrator.

I nod as I keep coughing, my hand to my throat.

“I’m sorry.”

We both turn in the direction of the male voice and see a dark-headed man jogging over to us.

Raquel is suspiciously silent as she hands me a bottle of water from her bag. I twist the cap off and take a drink as my breathing returns to normal.

"Sorry," he repeats as he approaches us. "My buddies don't have great aim." He smiles and reveals a set of straight, pearly white teeth. "Hi. I'm Jake."

I eye him from behind my sunglasses. If the frisbee had not taken my breath away, he definitely would have. He's tall, like Raquel, has jet-black hair and striking green eyes. They remind me of my mother's and for a moment, it's like I'm staring into hers again.

Raquel coughs, bringing me back into the moment and away from thinking about my mom. Jake turns to her and smiles again.

"Hi, Raquel."

"Hi, Jake," she says politely. "This is Thea. Thea, this is Jake Osborne."

"Thea," Jake repeats. I like how my name lingers on his tongue. "Pleasure to meet you. And again, sorry about the..." he trails off as he motions to his neck. He bends down and picks up the frisbee, never once breaking eye contact with me. He smiles and gives a little wave before tossing the frisbee to his group of friends and jogging back to them.

I stare after him and watch as he and his friends continue their fun.

"You good?" Raquel asks as she sits down on her towel and pulls out her own bottle of sunscreen.

"Uh, yeah," I mutter, forcing my eyes away from Jake. I lay my towel out beside hers and sit down while she coats her limbs in sunscreen. Freckles splatter her entire body. We sit in silence for a few moments before she declares she is going to take a dip. I hang back, digging my toes deep down into the sand. I lay back on my towel and let myself relax, my fingers fiddling with my necklace. I time my breathing to the sound of the ocean waves and for the first time in a while, truly feel at peace. It's in this moment that the voice in the back of my head verifies my decision to come to Driftbay. I never would have found this kind of peace in Seattle.

I lay there for a while, feeling the warmth of the sun wrap around me like a hug. I run my hands through the sand and come across a few lone seashells. I sit up and push my sunglasses into my hair to get a better look at them before I toss them into my beach bag.

I watch as Graham walks out of the water, surfboard in hand. My eyes drift back to Jake and his friends as Raquel frolics along the tide.

I shake my head to physically move my eyes off of him. *You don't have the capacity for a relationship right now,* I remind myself. I came to Driftbay to focus on myself and that's how it needs to stay.

But hey, it never hurts to look.

# Chapter Three

Beth

"So, what's going on with you and Charlie?"

I drop the plate I'd been washing. It clangs around the bottom of the sink, causing me to jump before the silence sets in. The longer I pause, the greater the implication of what I say next. Addressing Charlie to Thea means addressing to myself what we really are as well, and that's not a conversation I'm ready for on either account.

Charlie and I have never been on the same wavelength. He was my first friend when I moved to Driftbay thirty-five years ago, but we were young then and he was married to his high-school sweetheart. Later, they divorced but I was in a committed relationship at the time. And now...we tiptoe around the line between us, fearing fate tossing another obstacle in our way. It's just easier this way. No one gets hurt.

I've spent the majority of my adult life alone. I moved halfway across the country to go to college, away from my sister and our parents. I craved independence and moving far away seemed like the only way to get it. I majored in business and loved the area so much that I stayed after I finished school. I ended up opening the diner after graduation, much to my parents' dismay. Maybe dismay isn't the right word. I just know that they weren't exactly as proud of it as they were of my sister. Don't get me wrong; I know my parents loved me and were proud of me but there's just...well, the scales aren't weighted quite the same for a doctor and diner-owner..

I made a few other friends during my youthful years but once the diner really took off, I didn't really have time to do much else. I became married to the job. Girlfriends stopped coming by, boyfriends became nonexistent. All except for Charlie. Charlie stood by me through it all — a study partner on late-night review sessions in college, assisting with menu revisions, offering advice on what to serve at the diner (his favorite activity to help with), and helping vet applications when I needed to hire more people. To this day, he still sits in on interviews with me. It's just our thing. It's part of who we are.

Thea stares at me with a bewildered expression, the smirk on her lips growing stronger by the second.

"Charlie," I begin, unsure of how to divulge decades' worth of will they or won't they to her, "is my friend."

Simple enough. I leave it at that.

"OH-Kay," she replies in a mocking tone. It's obvious she doesn't believe me.

"Really," I double down.

"Mm-hmm." She gets up from the table and walks over to the sink, setting her dishes in the soapy water. "A friend doesn't look at you the way Charlie did this morning."

"What's that supposed to mean?" I let my hands rest in the warm water.

"I'm just saying," Thea begins. "He looked like he has it bad for you." She turns to leave.

I don't bother arguing with her. Instead, I start chewing on the inside of my cheek while I replay the morning's events.

Besides, how exactly do I explain that he's the right person, but we never got the timing right? Charlie and I have discussed our relationship long ago and come to the mutual realization that we're better off as friends.

I finish cleaning the kitchen and put the dishrag down on the counter before turning the light out. Grabbing my book, I head out to the porch and settle down into my chair. My bookmark falls out, but I don't pick it up. Instead, I flip through a few pages, not fully invested in the story, still thinking about Charlie and what Thea said. I can't concentrate no matter how hard I try. I give up on reading, knowing I'm not getting anything out of the words on the page. My mind whirls as I watch the sun go down and night fall upon the sleepy little town I call home. I finally relent and head back inside, unsure of the time. Thea's door is shut and I don't bother her. I start my evening routine, showering and skincare before getting into bed. Her words float through my mind on a loop and I spend the next couple of hours tossing and turning.

Part of me has always thought Charlie and I would end up together. Sort of like how people say they knew it was love at first sight. I knew from the moment he walked into English class during freshman year that he would be in my life in some capacity forever. But dating is messy, and feelings get hurt, and things can end badly. If having Charlie in my life as just a friend is all I get, I can be satisfied with that.

I stare at the ceiling for a while more before I finally succumb to another sleepless night. I get out of bed and return to the kitchen, flipping on the light as I enter. My eyes squint as they adjust to the brightness. I go to the pantry and retrieve the flour and sugar, my late-night friends. I close the pantry with the kick of my heel and grab the butter and eggs from the fridge. I set the ingredients down on the counter and roll up my sleeves before getting to work.

Baking has always been a source of comfort for me. When I was stressed about finals in high school and college, I baked. When I was worried about the diner in the beginning, I baked. When the jackass that broke my heart at thirty-two left, I baked. When Caroline died, I nearly turned the diner into a bakery. Baking has always been there for me when people haven't. I can twist and shape my feelings into something tangible that I can walk away from. It's my form of therapy.

I work until the wee hours of the morning, baking cookies and an apple pie to take to the diner later. I wipe at my brow with flour-covered hands as I lick the remnants of the pie filling from its mixing bowl while thinking about the day. I clean the kitchen up and package the desserts on serving trays, neatly tucking away my feelings with them. I know I'll regret the lack of sleep later, but for now my mind is clear. Feeling lighter and content, I shut the light off in the kitchen and retreat back to bed.

Charlie comes in for breakfast the next morning, just like he does every day. I serve him his usual and start to hear about his day at work before getting flagged down by one of my regulars. I hit my hip on the counter edge as I round it and grit my teeth as I approach Judith's booth.

"Yes, Judith?" I ask as I rub at the tender spot on my hip.

"Honey, could you grab me a slice of pie, please?" She stares up at me with watery dark blue eyes. Her silver and blonde hair is a coiled cuff around her head and she's dressed to the nines, sequins all over her top and bangles decorating her thin arms. She's spunky and feisty and my absolute favorite customer. Over the years, I've learned that she's a lifelong resident of Driftbay and has one son, who moved away once he hit eighteen. He doesn't visit often, so she is pretty lonely.

"Of course." I smile at her, the pain in my hip subsiding. "I'll be right back."

I head back to the counter, where Penny, one of my other waitresses, is making change for someone. She smiles at me as I pass her by and cut Judith a slice of apple pie. I cut an extra slice for Charlie and slide it over to him before I take Judith's slice back to her. Her hand shakes a bit as she picks up her fork, something I hadn't noticed before.

She smiles as she takes a bite and snickers as she puts the fork back down on the table. She brings a napkin to her lips.

"Oh, I'm being so bad!" she declares, dabbing at her bright pink lipstick. "But oh, the heart wants what the heart wants! Calories be damned. Honey, this is delectable."

"Thank you, Ms. Judith," I say.

Charlie catches my attention across the diner as he gets paged out on a call. I wave at him as he leaves. He nearly collides with Raquel as she barrels through the door. She's late and I know she hates being late. I watch as they exchange pleasantries and each go about their day. Raquel says hi to Penny before scurrying into the back room to get ready for her shift.

"Ms. Judith," I repeat as I slide into the booth opposite her. "Got any big plans for the day?"

"I'm going to get my hair done, dearie," she replies as she takes another bite of pie.

"Big day indeed." I smile as I watch her chew.

"How is that niece of yours?" she asks after she swallows.

"Thea?" I echo. Judith nods, urging me to continue, "She's good. I think she's adjusting to town nicely. She seems a bit happier here."

"Good. I'd like to meet her one day. If she's anything like you, I'm sure she's an absolute doll."

I smile at the compliment as I watch Raquel clock in at the register. She waves me down, getting my attention, and mouths 'sorry' across the restaurant.

Penny stops by the table to refill Judith's coffee — straight black, no sugar, no creamer. Just how she likes it. Penny is a newer waitress I hired on when Thea told me she wanted to come live with me. I figured I'd need the extra help once she arrived.

"Raquel and I switched shifts for tomorrow night," she tells me as she pours the liquid.

I nod. "As long as someone is here, I don't mind."

She beams. "Thanks, Beth. You're the best."

"I know," I laugh, "Now go check on table five." I nod my head in the direction of her section before turning my attention back to Judith.

"You've got good people here," she says. "Both staff and customers."

"I agree." I fiddle with her paper straw wrapper for a moment, wondering what she's getting at.

"How was Charlie this morning?"

"Good." My head snaps up at the mention of his name.

"Has he asked you out yet?" Judith asks.

"What?" I laugh, mostly out of nervous habit. "Why would he do that?"

Judith rolls her eyes and leans across the table. "Because he's a man and you're an attractive woman." She motions at me.

"Judith, you know as well as I do that Charlie and I are just friends," I say.

There's a twinkle in her eyes as she smirks at me. It reminds me of Thea the night before.

"Fine, fine," she says, putting her hands in the air. "I'll stop meddling. Just friends, you say."

The air is heavy between us as I repeat her words, "Just friends."

Maybe if I say it enough, I'll start to believe it, too.

Thea and I spend the evening after work making homemade pizzas together. I learn that, like her mother, she is not very adventurous with her toppings while mine is stacked high with green peppers, onions, and mushrooms. She tells me about her day, having spent it at the beach again. There's a tinge of red to her pale skin, no doubt the result of falling asleep on the beach. She is animated as she talks and I breathe a sigh of relief. For the last six months, she's had a black cloud hanging over her, a storm that wouldn't pass by. We make plans to go to the beach together over the next couple of days. I haven't had a proper beach day in ages.

We eat dinner quietly and watch the sunset from the porch before we both retreat to our respective bedrooms. I count my lucky stars that Thea is settling down well in Driftbay. It was a gamble when she said she wanted to move here with me. Part of me is worried that the solitude might worsen her depression, but so far it seems to be having the opposite effect. I can only hope it continues.

I go through my nightly routine — a scalding hot shower and skincare routine before changing into my favorite pajamas. I'm exhausted from not sleeping the night before and am convinced I'm asleep before my head hits the pillow.

It's around midnight when I wake up again. I get up to go to the bathroom and stumble around in the darkness. I'm still groggy when I return to bed but notice light spilling onto the floor from the kitchen. I must have forgotten to turn the light off, something I catch myself doing all the time. I rub at my eyes and yawn as I stumble down the hallway, sleep slowly loosening its grip on me.

Thea is in the kitchen at the sink. She's dancing around as she washes dishes and lip-syncing with a wooden spoon. She has headphones on, the big, over the head kind. She spins around, mouthing a high note and I can't help but laugh as I lean against the doorframe and watch her.

The timer on the counter goes off but she doesn't hear it. She's too busy lost in her own world. She opens her eyes and it takes a second for her to register that I'm standing in the doorway. She straightens up and rips the headphones off of her head.

"Sorry," she says, the carefree girl from moments ago vanishing before my eyes. "I didn't mean to wake you."

"You didn't," I say, pushing off the doorframe and walking over to her. "I woke up and saw the light on. I thought I'd left it on earlier."

A tray of brownies is cooling on the counter, steam rising from them as they cool. They look delicious. I can smell more in the oven and that reminds me that she didn't hear the timer.

"Your timer went off." I nod in the direction of it.

"Oh!" Thea grabs a couple of potholders and opens the oven, reaching for the second tray of brownies. She sets them on a cooling rack on the counter before adding, "I couldn't sleep and baking helps."

I remember right after Caroline died when she didn't sleep for three days. All the kid did was bake. She would barely talk to anyone, but everyone that came by to offer condolences was sent away with a baked good. She made muffins, scones, brownies, cookies, everything you can imagine. She didn't stop until I physically made her and then she collapsed in my arms and cried, finally letting her emotions out.

"You don't have to explain to me. I get it. Baking helps with my insomnia, too." I inhale the chocolatey aroma, twisting through the kitchen like ribbons in the air. "Those smell amazing. Kid after my own heart."

Thea beams. "I thought maybe you could take them to the diner in the morning. Share them with Raquel and Graham, and the rest of the staff. Maybe the customers, too."

"That's a great idea." I smile as she pushes up her sweatshirt sleeves. She goes back to washing her dishes and cleaning up as I add, "I'm going back to bed. I'll see you in the morning."

She nods as she washes a bowl. "Good night," she calls over her shoulder.

I watch her and feel my heart leap in my chest. I don't stop myself when the urge to hug her hits.

"'Night, kid." I kiss the top of her head before I turn and head back to bed.

Thea is asleep the next morning when I go to leave, but her brownies are neatly plated and covered in tinfoil, waiting for me on the counter. There's a note across the top of them, her neat handwriting scribbled across it.

*For being so kind to me,* she'd written.

I grab the plate and hurry out of the house. I've overslept and am running late. Graham and Raquel are off this morning but Brian and Penny will be there. Brian is another one of my cooks. He's good, not as good as Graham, but enough that it keeps my customers happy and coming back. Penny is sunshine in human form. I've only known her a short time but can already tell that she is a sweetheart and sees the absolute best in people. Charlie and I were both very pleased with her interview.

The drive to the diner is short and I park my car around back, in my usual spot. I hurry up the back steps, balancing the brownies in one hand, and flip the lights on as I enter. The diner springs to life before my eyes. Ah, my diner, my baby. I've poured my life into this place and don't know what I'd do without it.

Brian and Penny come in for their shifts not long after me and together, we get the diner ready to open. I like the routine of being at the diner every day. It gives me stability. Each day starts off like any other — bright and full of possibilities.

Charlie comes in not long after we open, as if right on cue, and starts to tell me what he can about his shift the day before. My attention is diverted when I see Graham come in and head towards the back room. He pops up by the counter a moment later.

"Morning, Graham," Charlie and I say in unison.

"Morning, Beth." Graham tips an imaginary hat to Charlie. "Morning, Sheriff Gajewski."

"How many times have I told you that you can call me Charlie?" Charlie's eyes glimmer and a smile tugs at his lips as I set a mug of coffee down in front of him.

Graham shrugs. "It's a respect thing. My mom always told me to respect men in uniform."

Charlie chuckles at his sincerity. "Your mom is a good woman," he says.

"What are you doing here?" I ask Graham. "You're not on until later this evening."

Graham waves a white envelope. "Wanted to pick up my paycheck and take it to the bank beforehand."

I nod.

"Is Thea coming by later?" Charlie asks me. I turn to look at him and notice Graham fumbling his check at the mention of Thea's name. Charlie and I both look at him as he not-so-gracefully tries to play it cool and knocks over a salt shaker on the counter.

"You okay there, son?" Charlie asks.

I put my hand on my hip as I wait for his response.

"Yeah," Graham says, stuttering a bit and looking at the floor.

"For a second, I thought you might have a crush on that girl."

Graham's cheeks start to turn a lovely shade of pink at Charlie's words.

"Charlie, stop," I mutter, suppressing a laugh. I look at Graham.

"Yeah, she's uh...she's cute or whatever."

I let my laugh out now. "Ask her to hang out," I tell Graham. "The worst thing she can say is no."

Graham nods slightly and then holds his check up again. "I'm gonna...go." He hurries past me towards the back room to exit out the back of the diner.

Charlie chuckles as he watches him and takes another sip of coffee as I set a plate of eggs and bacon in front of him.

"Anyway, back to your story," I tell him as I resume wiping down menus.

"Right. So, totally normal traffic stop," he begins, his eyes boring into me as if he can see to the depths of my soul, "this woman is *blasting* Silver Springs, just full on rocking out." He takes a bite.

"My favorite!" I exclaim.

He laughs. "I know, it made me think of you."

I smile as we sit in silence for a few moments, the only sound is the scraping of his fork against his plate.

"The car in front of her is a teenager and I barely get to the window before he gets out and just takes off on foot. Turns out, he had alcohol in the car and thought abandoning the vehicle was the better option. So, I take off after him and he turns down Main Street. Luckily, Stan was leaving that donut shop down there. You know, Joe's?"

I nod my head, hanging on his every word. His eyes sparkle, and I let myself wonder for a moment what it would be like if those eyes looked at me like that. To feel his eyes raking over my skin, drinking me in—

"Beth Ann," he says, and I'm snapped out of my trance.

"What?" I ask. I gently shake my head to get those thoughts out of it.

"You okay? You got quiet." Charlie's gaze is pensive now, searching my face for a hint of anything that is wrong.

"Yeah," I say, "I just got distracted." I wipe at a spot on the counter. I don't — *can't* — let him know what I'd been thinking about.

Or rather, fantasizing about.

"Anyway," he carries on, "totally ironic, right? A cop coming out of a donut shop. Stan sees us and takes off after us and ends up tripping on the sidewalk and fracturing his ankle." He shoves another forkful of food into his mouth, the amount on his plate disappearing at a rapid pace.

I've known Charlie long enough to know that Stan was his first partner on the force. He's considerably older than us and nearing retirement but still hanging on to the badge.

I feel my brows raise at his tale as I toss my dishrag over my shoulder. "Never a dull moment," I say. I smile back at him as our eyes lock and linger on each other for a moment.

The bell above the door rings and the moment is broken, over in a flash.

Charlie and I turn in the direction of it and see Judith walking in.

"Judith!" we yell in unison.

She beams and raises her arms in the air as she heads toward the counter. She's dressed in all sequins again today. I swear, all the woman owns are sequined and bedazzled tops.

She hops up onto the barstool beside Charlie instead of heading to her usual booth. For an elderly woman, she's quite agile.

"Any pie this morning, dearie?" she asks. Charlie looks at me now, eager at the mention of pie, as he finishes his eggs and bacon.

"No, actually," I begin, "but I've got something else for you two to try." I reach across the counter and pick up Thea's plate of brownies.

"Ah, new recipe?" Charlie asks, eyeing them. He leans closer on the counter to get a better look.

"You could say that." I take off the tinfoil and present the plate to both of them. They each select one, take a bite, and nod approvingly.

"Another winner," he says, crumbs spilling out of his mouth.

Judith nods her head in agreement. "You do have such a talent for baking, dearie."

"I didn't make these," I correct them. "Thea did."

"You Calloway girls sure can bake." Charlie pops the last bite of brownie into his mouth before he stands and stretches, tossing a ten dollar bill down on the counter. "Well," he says, "I've got to get back to the station and finish up on some paperwork. Beth Ann, excellent as always. Tell Thea those brownies were amazing. Judith, lovely as ever to see you."

"Will do." I nod my head as I watch him walk out the door before grabbing his plate, fork, and mug.

"Beth Ann," Judith says and it startles me. No one besides Charlie and my parents have ever called me by my full name.

"When are you going to throw caution to the wind and get you a piece of that?" she asks with a smirk and one raised eyebrow.

"Judith!" I swat at her with the dishrag from my shoulder and feel heat creeping into my cheeks. "We've talked about this."

"I am nothing if not persistent."

I nod my head. She's not wrong.

"Really, dearie, I'm not blind. He's in here every day. Surely, the man knows how to make his own eggs and bacon."

"Yes, but so are you," I counter.

"I don't seem to have a crush on you, now do I?" Judith stares at me while I offer no rebuttal.

"Charlie and I..." I trail off, watching the door he just exited through, "it's complicated."

"Lots of things in life are, dearie, but that doesn't mean you should immediately write them off."

I sigh and stare at her. "Why are you always right?"

She smiles. "I observe things and that man has it bad for you. He looks at you like you hung the stars."

"Thank you, Judith." I start scrubbing at the same imaginary spot on the counter again.

"Listen to me, Beth Ann." She leans across the counter as if she's telling me a secret, the bangles on her arms creating quite a symphony. "You're young. I don't want you to wake up one day at my age and realize that you never followed your heart and let yourself have what you truly want." There's a twinkle in her eyes.

"Thank you, Judith," I repeat. A smile tugs at the corners of my lips. I can't stay irritated at her for long.

She settles back onto her stool. "Look, Beth, just..." she trails off, "will you promise an old woman that you'll listen to your heart? Sooner rather than later?" she asks.

I stare at her, knowing she won't drop it until I promise.

"Fine," I say, letting go of the dishrag. I hold my right hand in the air as I swear, "I promise."

"Good. Now," she says as she smiles and reaches for my hands. She takes them between hers and pats them. "How about an omelette?"

I toss my head back with a laugh and then turn to the kitchen window. I get Brian's attention and relay Judith's usual order.

"Coming right up!" he yells before getting back to work.

I turn back to Judith in time to see her sly smile before she takes another bite of Thea's brownie.

Her words repeat in my head, and deep down, I know my heart wants Charlie.

# Chapter Four

## Thea

I have the dream again. In it, I re-live the accident that claimed my mother's life. Only this time, no one comes to save us. I watch as she slowly bleeds out in front of me, as she gasps her last breaths away, like a fish out of water. I keep screaming and screaming until there's no sound left at all, but no one can hear me. We're alone and no one comes to help.

I wake up in a cold sweat, gasping for breath and clutching the bedsheets underneath me. My eyes adjust to the darkness and I loosen my grip on the sheets; they're bunched beneath my fists. My heartbeat is racing as I shift to the side of the bed and stare out the window at the dark beach. I focus on my breathing to try and calm myself down. I'm surprised I didn't wake Beth up by actually screaming. Thunder claps in the distance and then, a strike of lightning appears, illuminating the night sky.

*It was just a dream,* I tell myself.

I've been having the same dream but with different variations for a while now. In them, the end result is always the same. I haven't told Beth about them. I don't want her to worry about me, at least, not anymore than she already does.

As much as I am enjoying my new life in Driftbay, the cost of it is not lost on me.

Some days I would do anything to turn back the clock. To have stayed home that day instead of dragging Mom out of the house. I think that's part of where my guilt comes from. Our excursion that fateful day was my idea. I wonder if she would still be alive if we had just stayed home. I've run away from Seattle and don't want to revisit, knowing it would be too painful to reopen those wounds. There are just moments when part of me wishes I could go back. A lot of the time I wish I could go back to being a kid. This is one of those times.

I was scared of thunderstorms as a child and I would give anything right now to be able to run into my mom's room and crawl into bed with her. To feel her wrap her arms around me, tell me it's all okay and going to be alright, and comfort me back to sleep.

But instead, I'm across the country, dreaming of her ghost.

The tears are silently streaming down my face as I look out the windows. My grief is like the ocean sprawled out in the distance. Calm at times, but it can also be raging, tumultuous, and hazardous depending on conditions. It ebbs and flows but it will pull me under if I get swept up in it.

Taking a shaky breath, I dry my face with my hands and wipe them on my leggings before I get up and make my way to the kitchen. Baking has become a nightly routine. I can fold and stir and whisk my feelings into whatever I'm concocting. It helps, taking those big, scary, overwhelming feelings and compacting them into something small and delicious.

I didn't sleep for three days straight after the accident. I think it was shock. Instead, I baked around the clock. I sent Ireland to the grocery store countless times whenever I'd run out of eggs or vanilla extract or anything else. I didn't know what to do with the grief that consumed me so instead I turned it into something I could hold. Something I could give other people. Something I could set down and walk away from. I didn't stop baking until Beth physically made me stop.

I open my bedroom door and listen for any sounds of her rumbling around the house. I'm always scared I'll wake her up, but it seems I'm in the clear. I quietly pad down the hallway toward the kitchen and flip the light on. It springs to life in the sudden brightness and I squint as my eyes adjust. The clock above the stove reads 1:32 a.m. I don't have a ton of time before Beth gets up for the morning shift so I decide to make something easy. A recipe I know by heart — my mother's favorite cake.

I retrieve the ingredients from the pantry and fridge and fall into auto-pilot mode as I work. What I would give to bake it again for her, to sing Happy Birthday in a horrendous off-key tone, and hear her laughter. The kitchen fills with the scent of artificial strawberries as the cake bakes, but to me, it's the sweetest scent I've ever known. If I close my eyes, I can almost imagine she's in the room with me, just within my grasp. I want to cry again, thinking of birthdays past, grateful I made them into celebrations when Mom didn't really want the attention.

While the cake bakes, I wash the dishes. The warm, soapy water feels comforting as I scrub at the mixing bowl. It makes me think of my childhood — Mom hated washing dishes so we ate mostly on paper plates when I was little. When I got older and could take on chores around the house, dishes became my duty. I've never minded them.

The timer rings to let me know that the cake is done baking. I pull it out of the oven, the steamy strawberry essence flooding my senses, hugging me. I set the cake pan on the counter and stare at it, thinking about all the love and heartache that I've baked into it.

I guess grief is just the price you pay for loving someone so much.

While it cools, I grab ingredients to make my signature vanilla icing. I grab my headphones from the counter and throw them on top of my head, putting on my favorite true crime podcast while I work. I mix the ingredients together, folding my melancholy in with each sweep of the whisk. It takes a while to get the icing to the *perfect* consistency and the cake has cooled enough by the time I get it done. I watch as the pink slowly disappears beneath the white and think about how it's like my life, in a way. Seattle was the pink, the base of my existence and Driftbay is the icing, the fresh, white new slate.

I think the insomnia is starting to get to me but at least I can breathe a little easier.

I lick the knife as I absentmindedly stare at my finished creation, hearing Beth moving around in her bedroom getting ready for work. I cover the pan with tinfoil before turning the kitchen light off, taking one last look at the cake on the counter.

"Happy early birthday, Mom," I whisper before going back to bed.

It's later in the day before I'm up and getting ready to go see Beth and her gang compared to my normal visits. I'd fallen asleep quite easily after I baked the cake and slept until noon.

Grief is a bitch. You think you're doing okay and then all of a sudden, it hits you like a wave, pulling you back under. It's always the little things that hurt the most. Like today — I was putting my necklace back on after I woke up, when all of a sudden, the chain snaps, sending the peridot stone scattering across the hardwood floor. It took me ten minutes to find it. I can replace the chain but it won't be the same. It's just another piece of her that's been taken from me.

My eyes are puffy from crying. I run my brush through my hair before pulling it back into a ponytail. I open the medicine cabinet and look for Beth's eye cream. I find it and gently dab some on my under-eyes. I throw on some shorts and a tank top before sliding my feet into socks and my tennis shoes. I stop in the kitchen and grab the cake before heading out the door.

The air feels muggy and clings to my skin as I begin the familiar trek to the diner, wrestling the cake pan in my arms. It's overcast today and the forecast is calling for rain — a storm is brewing on the coast. I mentally kick myself in the rear for not grabbing an umbrella before I left the house.

The parking lot isn't nearly as full when I round the corner today, probably because I'm not coming in during a rush. I jog up the few steps in the front and reach for the doorknob. I'm grateful Beth keeps the air so low in the diner — due to her hot flashes, she says — as I open the door and am blasted by a gust of cool air.

Raquel waves from across the diner as she heads to the counter for a drink refill. I trot over to my usual barstool and set the cake pan down. Penny is standing there wiping down menus.

"Oooh, what do you have for us today?" Raquel asks as she fills a glass full of ice water.

"Strawberry cake with vanilla icing." I take the tinfoil off and am dismayed to see that some of the icing is stuck to it.

Penny leans across the counter and slides her finger across the icing on the foil before bringing it to her lips. "Mmm," she mumbles as she tastes it. "Fabulous, as always."

"Thank you," I say, beaming.

"Graham, I have told you to keep that surfboard OUTSIDE! Seriously, you get sand everywhere with that thing!"

The three of us turn in unison in the direction of Beth's voice and see her chasing Graham through the restaurant towards the back room. He grins at us and waves as they barrel past us.

"Well," Raquel says, "Graham's here."

Penny laughs, as if she isn't stating the obvious.

"Are they always like this?" I ask, watching as Beth crosses the threshold to the back room behind him.

Raquel nods. "Pretty much."

We hear commotion in the back, the door slamming, and then Graham's voice declaring, "It's outside, it's outside!"

The two of them walk out of the back a moment later, Graham suppressing a grin and Beth looking aggravated. He's tying a black apron around his waist.

"Hey," I say as I meet Beth's gaze.

"Hi," she says, sounding a touch annoyed.

Graham looks up and smiles at me, causing the butterflies in my stomach to flutter unexpectedly.

Beth hurries off to take care of an elderly lady across the room. I observe her, taking in her sharp sense of style. She's in a bright pink bedazzled top and has bangles lining her thin arms. I think it's Judith. Beth has mentioned her eccentric style and dramatic flair before and this woman fits the description. Graham grabs a utensil packet from the back counter and unrolls it, taking the fork and stabbing it into the cake pan.

"Mmm." He nods approvingly after taking a bite. "Don't tell your aunt I said this," he says after he swallows, his voice low, "but this is way better than hers."

"Don't let her hear you say that," Penny warns, as if it's a competition between me and Beth.

Graham holds both of his hands up in the air and says, "Hey, just speaking the truth." He looks at his watch and adds, "Thea, it's great to see you again but I've got to get to work. Brian is going to kill me if I'm another minute late." He disappears into the kitchen, leaving Raquel, Penny, and I alone at the counter.

"I suppose I should get back to work, too," Raquel sighs. She looks around and sees one of her tables waving her down. "Duty calls," she adds as she pushes off the counter and takes off.

Graham appears behind the kitchen window and gives me a wave with his spatula. I find it endearing and offer a small wave back.

"So," Penny begins, "I'm having a pool party at my house tomorrow night. Just a small thing, a few of my husband's buddies and Brian, Graham, and Raquel. You are more than welcome to come, if you'd like."

"Yeah," I say. "That sounds like fun."

Penny opens her mouth to say something else but is interrupted when we hear Beth call my name.

She is sitting with the elderly woman now and they're waving me over. I hop off the barstool and cross the diner to them, taking a seat beside Aunt Beth in the booth.

"Thea," she says, "this is my good friend, Judith, that I've told you so much about. Judith, this is my niece, Thea."

Judith beams as she looks at me and reaches for my hands. She takes them in hers and pats them as she says, "Oh, dearie, it's so wonderful to finally meet you! Beth has told me so much about you."

I blush, meeting strangers always makes me anxious. Judith seems sweet and Beth has mentioned her enough times that I know she really likes her.

"How are you liking Driftbay?" she asks.

"I love it so far," I gush. "It's a lot different than what I'm used to, but I think I'm settling in nicely."

There's a moment of silence at the table for the unspoken reason of why I left Seattle.

"Are you still in college?" Judith asks.

I shift in the seat. "I dropped out last semester. It just...wasn't right for me at the time. Maybe I'll go back and finish one day."

Beth jumps in. "Thea's very bright, though."

Judith smiles. "That's okay, college isn't for everyone. Give yourself time to figure out what your heart truly wants." She leans across the table. "Do you have a boyfriend?"

"Oh my God, you don't have to answer her," Beth says.

"No," I laugh.

"Oh," Judith pauses, "You got a girlfriend?"

"Also no," I say.

"Nothing wrong with either." Judith leans back in her seat and looks at Beth. "What?" she asks. "Just trying to get to know her."

"You are insufferable," she laughs.

The bell above the front door dings and Beth glances in that direction. Seeing Charlie, she motions for me to get up so she can get out of the booth. She hurries over to him, well past his normal visit time as I sit back down with Judith.

"There you are," she says. "I was worried about you." She places a hand on her hip as they stand in the middle of the diner.

Charlie rubs his face, looking like he hasn't slept in days. "Had an early morning case I couldn't step away from."

"Come on, let's get you something to eat." Beth takes off for the back counter and Charlie slowly follows her to his usual barstool.

"That man," Judith mutters under her breath. She looks me dead in the eyes as she adds, "I don't know how, but we have got to get your aunt and that man together.

"Oh, so you've noticed it, too?" I ask.

"Noticed it?!" she gasps, stirring her coffee. "Honey, I may be old but I am certainly not blind."

I laugh out loud. I can see why Beth likes her so much. I tuck a strand of hair behind my ear as she adds, "I think the only two people who don't see it are Charlie and Beth themselves."

She's not wrong. Sometimes the people closest to a situation are the ones who can't see it for what it truly is.

"I keep telling her to go after what she wants, but she won't listen to me," Judith says, feigning annoyance. "It's simple, really. The heart wants what the heart wants."

"I doubt she would listen to me, either," I say. Aunt Beth is quite hardheaded.

"Well, let's brainstorm on it, alright, dearie?" Judith takes a sip of her coffee. "And come up with a plan."

I glance back toward Charlie and Beth. She's laughing at something he said and their heads are dangerously close together, as if they're sharing a secret at the counter.

"Thea," I hear. I turn around and see Penny at the counter, holding a glass of soda.

"I accidentally got root beer; do you want this?" she asks. She holds up the glass higher in emphasis.

"Sure," I say. I bid farewell to Judith and slide out of the booth to return to the counter.

Penny hands me the glass and I take a drink of it. The carbonation tickles my nose and I scrunch it as the bell above the door dings again.

Charlie and Beth pay no attention to us and Penny reaches for the plastic bag on the counter beside her.

"Hi," she says cheerfully as a customer walks up beside me. I turn to look and am surprised to realize it's Jake from the beach.

"Hi," he says, smiling at her as he reaches into his back pocket for his wallet.

“Two bacon cheeseburgers, fries, and a side salad,” Penny says, reading off the ticket from her notepad.

Jake nods and pulls some bills out of his wallet. He hands them to her and waits while she makes his change.

“Hey,” I say, getting his attention.

His green eyes slide over to me and it takes my breath away.

“Hi,” he says. I can tell he’s trying to place where he has seen me.

“Thea,” I say, trying to jog his memory, “from the beach.”

“Oh, right,” he says, shaking his head. “I remember now. The, uh, frisbee.” He gestures at his neck.

“Yeah.” I smile and feel a blush burn across my cheeks.

“How are you?” he asks. “Hopefully better than when my friends tried to annihilate you.”

“I’m good. How are you?”

Jake smiles again and I notice as his eyes dance over my body. “Better now,” he says.

Penny returns to the counter in front of us and hands Jake some dollar bills and coins. He gently takes them from her and slips them back into his wallet before returning it to his back pocket.

“So, Thea,” he says. “What do you say to getting dinner with me sometime?”

“Sure,” I say. “I’d like that.”

“Good.” Jake pulls his phone out and swipes at the screen. “What’s your number?” he asks.

I rattle off the digits and watch as he keys it into his contacts.

“How about Friday?” he asks.

I pretend to think about it, as if my schedule is jam packed. "That should work for me."

"I'll text you," he says as he locks the screen once more. He glances at Penny and nods at her. "Thank you," he says, grabbing the plastic bag off the counter. "Thea, I'll be talking to you later."

I nod in excitement as I watch him turn and head back to the door. I bite my lip as I swivel back to the counter on my barstool. Penny has vanished; off to tend to one of her tables.

This feeling is new. I've never been asked out before and never had much interest in dating, but Jake seems sweet and he definitely lucked out in the looks department.

After saying goodbye to Beth and Charlie and offering waves to Raquel and Penny, I head out of the diner. I feel like I'm floating as I start making my way back to Beth's cottage. So much so, that I don't even care that it starts raining halfway home and I end up soaked by the time I make it back.

The front door shuts gently behind me and I head down the hallway to my room for a change of clothes. I had planned to spend the day curled up on the porch, reading, but after a fresh set of dry clothes, I decide to call my best friend. I feel guilty that I haven't talked to her much since I moved.

Raindrops pound the windows and make for a soothing lullaby as I climb onto my bed and pick up the phone. I dial Ireland's number and put the phone to my ear, waiting to hear her voice.

"Hello?" she answers groggily, after the fourth ring.

Crap. She works the night shift and I'd forgotten about the time zone difference between us.

"Hey," I say, my breath catching in my throat, "is this a bad time?"

"No," she sighs, "I'm just annoyed."

"What's wrong?" I ask as I tuck my legs underneath me.

"Tucker's being annoying."

Tucker being her five year old miniature schnauzer. Ireland and I met during our junior year of high school when we both worked at the same little retail shop, specializing in home decor and clothing, and have been best friends ever since. There's nothing quite like working the same dead-end job that brings people together.

"So, how is Driftbay?" she asks. "Tell me everything."

"Well," I start, "I've made a couple of friends here. They all work in Aunt Beth's diner."

Ireland playfully sighs on her end of the line. "You're going to forget all about me."

I laugh. "I could never!"

"So, you've made friends. What are their names?"

I tell her about Raquel, Penny, and Graham. I also mention Charlie and Aunt Beth, and she's just as invested as Judith is now.

"I met a guy," I say, almost nervously.

"OH?" Ireland asks, her voice an octave higher. She was always pushing me to put myself out there and try to meet someone.

I nod, as if she can see me. "We met on the beach right after I moved here and then I ran into him again today and he asked me to dinner."

"That's exciting!"

"I don't know much about him, but I have a good feeling."

"I'm really happy for you. He better be a good guy," she says, "or I'll fly out there and beat him up myself."

I laugh and silence settles between us for a few moments.

"How are things back in Seattle?" I ask.

"Same as usual," she sighs. "I miss you."

"I miss you, too." I pause. "I've been baking again. I'm having a lot of trouble sleeping and have been missing Mom a lot lately."

"That's to be expected," Ireland says. "I can't even imagine. If something happened to my mom..." she trails off. "I wouldn't survive."

I tell her about the breakdown I had, courtesy of my necklace breaking. I eye the pendant sitting on my vanity as I tell the tale.

"You're being really strong," she says softly when I finish.

Everyone keeps telling me that. Ever since the accident, everyone keeps telling me how strong I am, but I don't feel strong. Most days, "being strong" feels more like a job I never applied for. I don't want to be strong. I want to set this grief down more than anything, but I don't know *how*.

"Thanks," I say with a sigh.

We sit in silence again for a few moments before I hear a crash in the background and she tells me she has to go. We hang up and I'm left alone with my thoughts. The hum of the air conditioner keeps me company as my eyes settle on the calendar on the opposite side of the room.

The date stares back at me as if it has a flashing neon sign around it. June thirteenth is in two days, marking six months exactly since the accident...and my mother's birthday.

I know her birthday will be hard. Mother's Day was hard enough to face without her. I'm not prepared for her actual birthday.

Every Mother's Day, we would go to her favorite restaurant for lunch and then spend an afternoon picking out flowers to decorate our porch with for the summer. She loved gardening and said it was a great stress reliever for her. She adored mixing and matching different plants and flowers, turning our porch into a jungle oasis for the summer months.

This year, I spent the day alone. I did not get brisket for lunch. I did not help pick out flowers, nor did I push a cart overflowing with plants and flowers. Instead, I spent some time at the hospital where she worked, and with their permission, scattered some of Mom's ashes along their small garden by the cafeteria. I packed boxes to prepare for the move, reducing a lifetime of memories into a few cardboard boxes.

I keep trying not to think about her birthday. There will be no cake baked, no horrendous off-key singing, no special presents opened, no home full of laughter. If I ignore it long enough, the calendar will just skip it and it'll be a normal day.

Except it can't be a normal day. I can't just skip it. I have to face my mother's birthday alone.

Of course, I know I'm not really alone. I've got Aunt Beth, Ireland, Raquel, and Penny. Heck, even being around Charlie, Judith, and Graham at the diner is enough to lift my spirits.

But still...her birthday looms and it puts ice in my veins. It makes me scared that I'll never feel the sun again.

Beth and I are up early the next morning, preparing for our beach day. She packs a cooler full of water bottles, fruit, various snacks, and sub sandwiches. I grab our sunhats and the bottle of sunscreen. Really, we don't need to pack as much as we do — we could always run back up to the house if we needed anything. I just don't think either of us wants to run back and forth all day.

Wooden planks creak under our feet as we trudge out to the beach. When we reach the end of the boardwalk, I reach down and kick off my sandals, letting my feet sink into the sun-warmed sand. I keep sinking as I walk, lugging the cooler along with me as I follow after Beth. She's headed towards the water with our umbrella thrown over her shoulder and chairs in her other hand. It's a perfect day for a beach trip — the sun is shining brightly and glittering off the water, it's warm, but there's a nice breeze. The seagulls are chirping happily overhead, as if they're trying to talk to me.

Beth finds a spot she deems acceptable and sets our chairs down. She kicks off her sandals and lets her toes settle into the sand before she decides to tackle securing the umbrella.

I straighten my chair out and throw my towel over the back of it and set the cooler down between us as a makeshift table. Beth wrestles the umbrella deeper into the sand.

"There," she says, wiping at her brow. It's beyond hot out already. She tests the umbrella to see how far it will give and once she is satisfied, fixes her own chair and sits down.

There's quite the crowd on the beach already today. Someone is blasting music from a speaker down the beach, but I can't make out the words.

"This is nice," Beth murmurs as she stares out at the water.

"It is," I agree.

"I couldn't tell you the last time I got out here," she says quietly.

"A shame," I say, sliding my sunglasses over my eyes and reaching for the bottle of sunscreen. If I had lived here as long as Beth has, I'd have made it a point to be out on the beach at least three times a week.

"Life just happened." She shrugs. "I got busy and time just got away from me."

"I guess it does make it harder, being out here by yourself and with the diner." I coat my arms in sunscreen and hand the bottle to her.

"Speaking of the diner," she says cautiously as she rubs sunscreen on her legs, "I've been thinking. I was wondering if you'd like to become a more permanent part of the diner."

"What do you mean?" I ask.

"I want you to take over the baking."

"Really?" I can't believe what she is saying.

"I think it would be good for you," she says. "Give you something to do, help develop a routine. Besides, you're there every day anyway and everyone seems to love you."

"Yeah," I agree, feeling a flutter of excitement. "I think you're right."

"Great." She smiles and breathes a sigh of relief. "I kind of already told everyone you'd be joining us."

"Good thing I said yes," I laugh.

"We could start out with a couple of days a week and see how it goes, then go from there. I mean, you're supplying all the baked goods right now anyway. Charlie and Judith agree, too."

My ears perk up at the mention of Charlie as she sets the sunscreen bottle on the cooler between us.

"Charlie," I say mischievously. "How is ole Charlie?"

"He's fine."

I smirk at her as she says nothing more. "Oh, come on," I say, "nothing more than that?"

"I've told you, Charlie and I are just friends," she says.

"That's not what Judith thinks," I shoot back.

Beth's mouth drops open a little and then she frowns. "Since when have you talked to Judith about Charlie and I?"

"I'll tell you my secret if you tell me yours." I feel like a little kid again, taunting her.

"There is no secret!" she declares, raising her hands in defeat.

"Whatever you say. You look at him like he hung the moon."

"Oh, I do not," she scoffs. "Charlie and I are just friends and that's all we'll ever be."

I can see the hint of blush creeping into her cheeks and decide I've done enough teasing.

"I have a date tomorrow night," I say, changing the subject.

"Really?" Beth's head jerks in my direction. "With Graham?"

"What? No," I say, furrowing my brows.

"Oh." She frowns.

"Why did you think it was with Graham?"

"No reason," Beth says, a little too quickly.

I narrow my eyes as I look at her but decide not to press the issue. "A guy named Jake," I say.

"Sounds familiar," she murmurs.

"I met him that day I went to the beach with Raquel and Graham. Ran into him when his friends accidentally threw a frisbee at us."

Beth nods. "Sounds fun," she says. "I don't know if I'm supposed to give you a curfew or not. I mean, you're an adult, but still."

I laugh and shuffle in my chair. "Mom would want you to."

"Then how about midnight?"

"Sounds reasonable." I nod slowly, as silence settles between us. I watch as the other families on the beach laugh and play together. Ghosts of trips' past play out in my head, of Mom, Beth, and I on the beach when I was little. Mom and I building sandcastles together, hunting for seashells, splashing Beth in the water...

*Mom sits next to me in the sand in an abstract-printed blue bathing suit, a pop of color against her sun-kissed skin. She's helping me build a sandcastle. A gust of wind blows through and her sunhat goes tumbling off of her head; she catches it from mid-air. I laugh with delight as she makes a show of shoving it back down on her head. I have a mermaid Barbie in one hand, playing around the castle Mom is molding. Aunt Beth is down at the water's edge, looking for seashells for me.*

*"Only the prettiest shells for the princess," she says.*

*Mom has a cooler packed with all of my favorite snacks and drinks. I huff and puff as she makes me reapply sunscreen, letting her rub the coconut-scented lotion into my skin. She pays extra attention to my face and kisses the top of my head before she lets me run wild and join Aunt Beth at the edge of the water. She scoops me into her arms and I giggle as her bag of shells conduct a symphony at her hips.*

*Mom smiles as she watches us and walks over to join us. Aunt Beth sets me down in the sand and each of them takes one of my hands, swinging me as we walk along the tide. I take a few cautious steps into the water.*

*"Don't go too far, Thea," Mom warns.*

*The water is warm underneath my feet and I wiggle my toes in the wet sand. I crouch down to look at a shell and an incoming wave knocks me over.*

*"Thea!" Aunt Beth shouts as she bends down to scoop me up.*

*I'm a mess of giggles, saltwater, and sunscreen as she and Mom attempt to grab my hands but I splash at them. They start laughing and splash me back in return.*

A seagull chirps somewhere nearby and the memory vanishes.

"So," I clear my throat, not wanting to approach the subject but knowing I need to, "do you realize what tomorrow is?"

Beth nods solemnly. "I do. I wasn't sure if you'd want to talk about it or not."

I watch a wave roll in before I speak again. "Not really," I sigh, "but we probably should."

"She wouldn't want you to be sad."

"I know. I just can't help it." I stare at the water.

"I told everyone at the diner I wasn't coming in so I could be with you," she says softly.

I look over at her. "Thanks," I say. "I really appreciate that."

"You're welcome." Beth nods. Then silence grows between us, interrupted only by the sound of the waves crashing to shore. Another one rolls back out, taking our conversation with it.

I arrive at Penny's house for the pool party at the same time as Graham. He smiles and waves at me as he slams his car door shut, a beach towel tossed over his shoulder. I shift on my feet as I wait for him to get closer, slinging my bag onto my shoulder. I had almost not come to the party. It had been a fun, but emotionally day at the beach with Aunt Beth.

"Hey," he says as he reaches my side.

"Hi," I echo back as we walk up the sidewalk to the front porch together.

"Beth told me you're joining the crew at the diner," he says, running a hand through his hair.

"Yeah, she talked to me about it this morning. Good thing I said yes." A big smile spreads across my face. "I'm really excited."

"Well, we're excited to have you on board." He clears his throat and reaches into the pockets of his neon swim trunks.

"I, uh," he pauses as he pulls something out, "found this the other day and it made me think of you." He holds out his hand and in the center of his palm is a seashell in the shape of a heart.

"Graham," I say quietly, taken aback by the gesture. I gently reach for the shell and take it from him, running my fingers over the grooved surface. It's white and weathered and I know I will cherish it.

I open my mouth to continue but am interrupted by Penny answering the door.

"Hi!" she exclaims as she welcomes us into her home. Her home is warm and inviting; it's the kind of house that isn't perfect and looks lived in. There're toys spread across the living room and a cozy lamp lit in the corner. Her couch looks like a giant marshmallow.

Raquel smiles and waves to us from the kitchen as she watches us walk in. A few other people I don't know are in the house as well. I chalk them up to being Penny's husband's friends.

Graham departs from my side, going to talk to Brian and Penny's husband. I make my way over to the kitchen to join Raquel, saving my introductions for later. The kitchen is beautiful and spacious, everything a pristine white. Penny follows behind me.

"Make yourself at home," she says as she opens the fridge. "There's seltzers on the counter, help yourself."

Raquel nods and holds hers up.

"Oh, I'm not legal yet," I say, as I set my beach bag on the counter and take a seat at one of the barstools in front of it. I reach inside for my pouch of shells — still full from my beach day with Beth — and carefully slide Graham's shell into it.

"We're all legal here." Penny turns around, a meat and cheese tray in her hands. She shrugs. "Seriously. We won't tell."

She sets the food down and then takes off again, fluttering around like the social butterfly she is.

Raquel takes a drink of her seltzer and smiles at me. "Beth told me you're joining us at work," she says. "I'm so excited!"

"That's what Graham said," I say. "Did she make an announcement or something? She was banking on me saying yes," I laugh. News of me joining the crew has spread like wildfire, it seems.

She shrugs. "Kind of. I think she's just excited, too, so she wanted to tell everyone." Her eyes land on my bag and she frowns.

"Crap," she mutters, "I forgot my bag in my car. Be right back!" She scurries off to the front door and I turn around on the barstool and take a look around the house.

It's the kind of house where all the kids would hang out. Part of me always wished our apartment back in Seattle was the hotspot.

Thinking of home makes my heart hurt and I blink rapidly to fight the tears that are coming.

Everyone seems to have an alcoholic drink of some sort in their hands. I turn back around and stare at the seltzers curiously before I reach for one. I want to get rid of this lump in my throat. I crack it open and take a sip. It's not what I expect, but it's also not bad. I keep drinking it as I look around the kitchen. There's music playing from somewhere in the house and I can tell Penny is enjoying her role as hostess. There's a variety of finger foods spread across the counter, and a stack of pizza boxes by the fridge. I finish the can and toss it into the trashcan by the corner of the counter and reach for another. I crack it open and take a sip, feeling a numbing sensation working its way over my brain.

I decide not to wait for Raquel and head out the sliding glass door to the porch overlooking the pool. I set my bag down on one of the chairs on the deck and quickly strip my clothes off. I stuff them into my bag and drape my towel over the back of the chair. I take another gulp of my seltzer and set it down by the chair, feeling warm in the pit of my stomach. The lump in my throat is fading.

The pool looks inviting and refreshing after the day I've had. The smell of chlorine hits me in the face as I take a breath in. I hear a roar of laughter inside the house and pick up my seltzer can again, taking another drink. I quickly drain the can and crush it, setting it by my bag. Raquel joins me on the porch, shutting the patio door behind her. She smiles as she yanks her T-shirt over her head and shimmies out of her shorts, revealing her black bikini. She balls her clothes up and tosses them toward the chair beside me. She chucks her bag in the same direction and then walks toward the pool entrance and dips her toes in, testing the water.

"Cold?" I ask as I watch her.

"Not really," she says before she climbs in.

I walk to the pool ladder and follow her into the water. I shiver a bit as I adjust to the temperature. It's still early enough in the season that it's not turned to bath water just yet. I submerge myself fully and shake my head when I break the surface again. My mind is quiet and for once, I feel totally relaxed. It's a peace I could use more often.

I'm wiping water from my eyes as I remember I wanted to tell Raquel about Jake asking me out. She's on the other end of the pool, floating on her back, eyes shut. I swim over to her and settle beside her as Penny, Graham, and the others walk out onto the deck.

Graham rips off his shirt and breaks out into a run, jumping into a cannonball.

I turn, trying to shield myself from the spray. "I forgot to tell you," I say to Raquel after the water settles, "I saw Jake again and he asked me out."

"And you said no, right?" She flips out of her suspended float and is upright, in front of me.

"No..." I trail off, backing towards the edge of the pool. I furrow my brows as I look at her.

She frowns. "Look, I'm not telling you what to do, but be careful," she warns. "He may be nice now, but the kid is a real ass, at least from what I've heard around town."

"Really?" I ask, thinking of my interactions with Jake. "He seems sweet, so far."

"That's how they get you," she says, "Look, Thea, you're a big girl and can make your own decisions. Just be careful, okay?"

She glances toward Graham as he bobs along the surface of the water, slowly swimming over to us.

"Hey," he says, "whatcha talking about?"

"Just how excited we are to have Thea join the diner," she lies.

Graham agrees with her and I smile politely, lost in my thoughts. I think of his gesture at the door with the shell and now Raquel's warning. I can't help but wonder if I'm about to make a huge mistake.

I wake up the next morning filled with dread. I stare at the ceiling for a considerable amount of time before I make myself get up and get on with the day. I'd be content to lay there the entire day, but I know I need to get up and move my body.

Part of me thought this day would kill me. That somehow, grief would just take me in my sleep and I'd never have to face it.

Unfortunately, I'm still here, even though Mom isn't.

It's quiet in the house as I move about it, so I figure Beth is out on the porch reading or just watching the water. I busy myself with taking a quick shower. I put on a fresh set of clothes and head towards the kitchen to attempt to eat breakfast.

I feel like I'm having an out of body experience today. My heart feels heavy and my brain feels like a sponge — except serotonin is the water and I'm in a drought.

My phone buzzes in my hand as I walk down the hallway to the kitchen. I glance at it; it's Ireland. Just a heart emoji, her version of a "thinking of you" text.

A tear slides out of my eye and I brush it away as I flip the kitchen light on. There's a piece of paper in the center of the table and I walk over to see Beth's handwriting scribbled across it.

*Emergency at the diner. I'm so sorry. Be back as soon as I can! Xoxo*

Great. The one day I didn't want to be alone and I'm left utterly and completely alone.

I toss her note back on the table and slowly walk over to the refrigerator. I open it and grab the carton of eggs and butter. I'm in a daze as I retrieve the flour and sugar from the pantry.

I bake chocolate chip cookies and a loaf of banana bread in an attempt to feel better. I've just finished washing the dishes when the timer for the banana bread goes off. I pull it out of the oven and set it on the cooling rack on the counter. It smells divine, but I frown at it anyway. I don't feel the relief that usually comes with baking.

This is the first time that baking hasn't helped. I tell myself that I just need to bake *more*; eventually it will take the pain away. I just need to fold my grief in more tightly, to whisk it into oblivion.

I go back to the fridge and open it, staring at its contents. There's not much to work with, we need to get groceries again. I'm staring at the food inside, running recipes over in my mind when my eyes land on a bottle of vodka at the back of the top shelf. I reach for it, hands shaking as I grasp it and pull it forward.

I think of Penny's words yesterday. *"We're all legal here."* How nonchalant she was about it and how no one seemed to bat an eye at my age.

I unscrew the cap and take a whiff. I recoil in disgust, unsure how anyone could drink this stuff. I glance over my shoulder to make sure I'm alone and then I take a gulp.

It burns all the way down. A fiery warmth lands in the pit of my stomach and I gag at the after taste.

And yet...I don't stop.

I take another mouthful and swallow it down, washing my sadness away with it. The liquid warmth starts to spread through my entire body, melting the ice from my veins.

I look back in the fridge for something to chase it with. I spot a lone bottle of Gatorade and grab it, twisting the cap off and taking a sip.

There. That's better.

I know I shouldn't be doing this, but I'm hurting and baking isn't enough to numb the pain today.

Beth would be livid if she knew, that much is certain. I just can't help myself. I keep drinking gulp after gulp until the bottle is empty and the pain is temporarily gone.

*Now you've done it,* I think to myself. I can't just toss the bottle away, Beth would surely notice that. I can't go out and purchase a new one for her, either. My best option is to run it full of tap water and pray she doesn't reach for it often. I messily gauge how full the bottle was when I started and run it under the tap. My head is starting to spin and I don't know whether it's from the vodka or my thoughts.

I leave the bottle on the counter and pull my phone out of my back pocket before I sink down to the floor. Tears start spilling out of my eyes as I lean against the cabinets.

Shakily, I scroll through my contacts until I reach the one number that hasn't been answered for months. I press on it and bring the phone to my ear, listening as it rings.

"Hello, you've reached Dr. Caroline Calloway. I can't come to the phone right now, but if you leave your name and number, I'll return your call as soon as I can."

The tears are falling faster now as I listen to my mother's voice. I end the call and toss my phone aside, letting my shoulders shake as sobs rack my body. I press a hand to my mouth to stifle my weeping, not wanting to be heard, though I'm alone in the house. I can feel snot running out of my nose and I wipe at it with my sleeve before I pick up my phone again. I redial the number and listen as it goes to voicemail again.

"Hi, Mom," I say, my voice shaking. I sniffle. "I miss you. It's your birthday and I just want to be able to hug you. To tell you I love you. For you to be here with me and Aunt Beth. She misses you, too, by the way, but she's stronger about it than I am." I pause and take another trembling breath. "I really, really miss you. I'm sorry I drug you out of the house that day. Maybe you'd still be here if it weren't for me."

I sit there, clutching my phone in one hand, sobbing on the kitchen floor. I lean over onto my side and curl into the fetal position, thinking about the wreck.

"I've been baking," I whisper into the phone, "but it doesn't help. Nothing helps. It hurts all of the time and I don't think it will ever stop. I wish you were here to tell me what to do. You always knew what to do and I-"

The voicemail clicks off and the call disconnects, shutting me up. It makes me cry even harder; just another instance of my mom being taken from me. There wasn't enough time on the voicemail; there's never enough time.

I'm not sure how long I lay on the tile floor, but it feels cool against my flushed, tear-stained cheeks. Somewhere in the back of my brain, something tells me to get up. That it would break Beth to walk in on me like this. She's been so strong since Mom died and I know she worries about me. My brain repeatedly tells me to get up, but it takes me a while before I actually am able to push myself up off the floor. My head still spins as I sit up and close my eyes as I take a deep breath. I stand up and wipe at my face, grabbing a napkin off the counter to blow my nose with while staring at the vodka bottle on the counter. I replace the bottle in the fridge and shut the door.

I just want to bury myself in my bed and go to sleep, because when I sleep, I don't have to feel this pain.

Turning off the kitchen light, that's exactly what I go to do.

# Chapter Five

## Thea

Jake is ten minutes late for our date the next night.

My stomach is in knots while I wait for him outside of Beth's house. Before the accident, I didn't bat an eye if someone was late for plans we'd made. I just figured they'd run into traffic on their way or misjudged the time. Now, my anxiety expects the worst — thinking I will hear that they, too, have been involved in a life-changing accident.

I hear a motorcycle off in the distance, getting louder as it seems to get closer to the house. It turns down our road and then into Beth's driveway.

Jake removes his helmet and smiles as he sees me. He is clad in black jeans, boots, and a black leather jacket. It melts some of my anxiety away. He's here, he's safe, and everything is okay...until I realize that his motorcycle is our method of transportation for the night. He didn't mention that when he'd text me about tonight.

"Hey, Thea," he says, before offering me the extra helmet from the back of his bike.

"Hi," I say, finding my voice as I walk towards him. The gravel driveway crunches under my feet, my footing a bit unsteady in my sandals. The knots in my stomach tighten at the thought of riding on the back of his motorcycle.

"Can we walk?" I ask, eyeing the helmet in his gloved, outstretched hand.

"Nah," he says, urging me to take the helmet. "It's only, like, a five minute drive. You scared?" He smiles that wonderful smile that makes me weak in the knees.

He's only teasing, of course, so I don't tell him that yes, I am scared.

"We could get our steps in if we walk," I say, a stupid attempt at a joke. I'm starting to panic and am grappling at anything.

"I'm not walking," Jake says. He's more assertive than I've seen him before. "It's really not that far. You'll be fine. People ride on my motorcycle all the time. Seriously, Thea, you're not gonna die."

"I just don't feel comfortable," I start, images of the car crash flooding my brain.

"Hey," Jake says, sensing that I'm panicking.

My eyes fly open and I stare at him, smiling at me. "I've got you. I'll protect you. You can trust me."

I open my mouth for a rebuttal but he stops me.

“I’m not walking,” he repeats. “So, you can either ride on the motorcycle or I guess we end the evening right here.”

I reach for the helmet reluctantly. I just want him to like me. He kicks the kickstand down and swings his leg over the bike. He comes around to help me put the helmet on. Our eyes linger on each other for a moment before he brushes my hair off of my shoulder. I shiver at the contact, goosebumps decorating my skin.

“Atta girl,” he says quietly before he turns back to the bike, motioning for me to follow him. He mounts it, steadies it, and looks at me again.

“Put your foot here,” he says, guiding me to the pillion peg, “and your arm here.” He moves my hand to his bicep. “Step up, put your weight on me, and swing your leg over.”

I do as he says and toss my leg over the side, thanking my lucky stars that I wore jeans instead of a dress. It’s an awkward movement as the bike wobbles a bit but I sit, settling against the seatrest. Jake steadies the bike and gets situated.

I catch a whiff of cigarette smoke from the back of his jacket and grimace. He turns the key in the ignition and the motorcycle revs back to life. The sound of it makes me want to crawl out of my skin.

“Hold on tight,” he says as he starts to back down Beth’s driveway. I wrap my arms around him to hold on for dear life as he pulls out onto the main road. I shut my eyes as he quickly gathers speed and feel him dart in and out of traffic on the main road.

“Can you slow down?” I yell, my hair whipping all around me.

"What?" Jake yells back over his shoulder.

I open my eyes as he zig-zags lanes again. He's being a reckless driver and I know how this can end. I want off of this bike before he wrecks it. My stomach rolls again as I watch Driftbay pass by in a blur.

He drives us to a less-than-picturesque little dive bar tucked away on the edge of town. There's a wooden sign with chipped paint standing tall and proud outside and I can barely make out that we're at The White House Tavern.

Weeds have grown up around the foundation of the tavern, looking messy and unkempt. There's a neon sign in the dirty window that flashes 'open' every few seconds. Jake parks his motorcycle across the street and gently helps me off of it. I rip the helmet off of my head and smooth down my hair, grateful to be on solid ground again.

He doesn't say a word as he leads me toward the tavern, up a rickety wooden wheelchair ramp to the front door. It's decorated in handwritten signs displaying various specials. We walk inside, the bell above the door ringing through the silence between us. There's mismatched diner booths lining the wall, some looking well past their prime with rips and tears in their lining. Christmas lights adorn the walls, even though it's June. There's a bright fluorescent light overhead and I squint as I glance around. A few tables are scattered about, with varying styles of chairs accompanying them. It doesn't look like anyone gave the interior design of this place any thought, just threw together what they could find or salvage. The air is thick as we make our way down a couple steps into a lower-level of the bar. There's one bartender behind the counter in the main room, a girl that looks to be around my age — young and blonde. I don't miss how Jake seems to check her out as we pass by, noticing how he sucks his breath in and lets out a low whistle. I spot a couple of slot machines in the far-right back corner, a designated gambling corner. Their neon lights shimmer like a lighthouse to a lost ship at sea. There's a couple of older men sitting in front of them, pressing their luck and hoping to win big.

The floorboards creak underneath my feet as Jake heads to a table in a secluded, dimly-lit corner. He pulls out his chair before he takes off his jacket and slings it over the back.

Hardly the place I would have picked for a first date.

I pull my own chair out after a moment, realizing he isn't going to touch mine. I take my phone and wallet out of my pocket and set them down on the table as I sit down and scoot closer. The table feels sticky and gummy, the kind you get when the varnish never fully dries.

I pick up the laminated menu and start to peruse it as Jake asks, "Do you want a drink?"

"Oh," I say, looking up at him. "I'm not twenty-one yet."

He leans forward, smirking. "I didn't ask if you were twenty-one. I asked if you wanted a drink."

"Sure," I say, after a moment. "I'll just have whatever you're having." Alarm bells are going off in my head but I ignore them, deciding to give him a chance to prove them wrong.

Jake gets up and heads to the bar. I take a deep breath and visualize the knots in my stomach unraveling in an attempt to calm my nerves.

He's not gone very long before he returns with our drinks in hand. He sets a bottle of beer down in front of me and returns to his chair, tipping his own bottle back.

"So, you've just moved to Driftbay?" he asks, leaning back in his chair.

I nod, bringing the beer to my lips. I take a sip and cough, disgusted at the taste. I set it back down on the table and gently nudge it toward him. "I'm originally from Seattle. I wanted to come live with my Aunt Beth. You might know her, she owns Beth Ann's Diner here in town."

"Yeah, I know her." He nods.

Of course. I should have known. Everyone in Driftbay knows Beth.

"Why would you want to leave Seattle and come to this craphole?" he asks.

"I don't think it's a craphole," I argue. Driftbay has been a blessing to me, a bright spot in an otherwise dark time in my life.

"There's not much to do here," he says, taking another swig of his beer. "It's a dead-end town full of meaningless jobs. There's so much more room to grow in Seattle, opportunities to make something of yourself."

He talks like he's been there before. I don't ask him if he has. I frown and think of Beth, and her success with the diner. I wouldn't necessarily call that a "dead-end".

"So," I say in an attempt to change the subject, "have you always lived here?"

He nods. "My dad is James Osborne." He says it like I'm supposed to know the importance behind the name.

There's a beat of silence between us before I laugh softly, saying, "Sorry, I'm still learning everyone's names. I don't think I've met him yet."

Jake laughs now. "You won't, unless you're in a courtroom."

I stare at him, still not quite following what he's saying.

"He's the best attorney in town," he says, "The 'silver-tongued king of the courtroom' as the newspaper says."

I nod slowly.

"You want my family on your side." Jake leans closer across the table. "My father can ruin anyone in this town."

"Duly noted," I say.

The bartender appears at the edge of our table and I'm grateful for the distraction. She smiles as she takes out her notepad and a pen.

"Hi," she says, "I'm Emily and I'll be taking care of you guys. Can I get you any appetizers?"

I glance back at the menu as I hear Jake say, "Hi, Emily," rather sweetly.

"I'll just have a burger and fries," he adds, "Extra onion."

I hastily order some nachos and hand the menu back to her as Jake takes another drink, draining his beer.

"Do you want another beer?" she asks.

He nods.

“I’ll be right back.” Emily turns around and heads back to the counter, ringing a bell and throwing our order in the kitchen window as she passes.

Not quite the service I’m used to at the diner.

"So,” I say after a moment of silence. “Do you work?”

Jake nods. “I help around my dad’s office from time to time.”

“I’m starting soon at the diner,” I offer, glad we’re getting to some common ground. “I like to bake so Aunt Beth is going to have me do the baking there.”

“I’d like to try something some time,” he says as he reaches across the table for my hand and I get a glance of the guy I saw in the diner. His thumb brushes over my knuckles and I feel the knots in my stomach morph into butterflies.

“Maybe I could bake for you some time.”

“I’d like that.”

“What’s your favorite dessert?” I ask as Emily returns with another beer for him. She sets it down wordlessly and leaves us be.

“Favorite dessert,” he muses, leaning back in his chair again. He strokes his chin as he ponders his response. “Probably Baked Alaska.”

“I’ve never made that before, but I’m always up for a challenge!” I have to admit, I’m excited at the prospect.

Jake smiles again and then goes on to tell me he’s in a band, he plays the guitar, and is also a backup singer. He mentions that they’ve had a gig at this bar before and becomes animated as he talks about the band with his cousin. For a moment, I consider coming to watch them play.

Our food arrives shortly after that. It's quiet between us as we eat, except for the sound of the slot machines across the room and the radio blaring old country music. The food is surprisingly good for a dive bar. Jake devours his burger and fries and is getting a third beer before I've even made a dent in my nachos. I resign myself to the fact that I'll be walking home based on how many beers he's downing.

Emily appears again, her notepad in hand.

"Is this together or separate?" she asks, clutching her pen in her right hand.

I open my mouth at the same time Jake opens his.

"Separate," he declares and I feel my mouth turn sour.

I offer a small smile at Emily before she turns around to go split our check. I glance back at Jake, feeling slightly off-put after the night's turn of events. He's picking at his teeth now with a toothpick from the table and staring across the room at Emily's ass as she walks.

I'm ready for this night to end. Jake is not my knight in shining armour, though I'd thought for a moment that he might be.

Emily returns with our checks and we pay our respective bills. I see something written in red on his and make out a phone number. Emily's.

Jake stretches as he stands and I jump up, ready to start heading home.

"Well," I say, "this was...fun." I smile at him, even though my blood is starting to boil. I clutch my phone and wallet in one hand before shoving them into my pocket. Just as I'm starting to step around him, he reaches for my wrist and spins me back to face him.

"Party's not over yet, is it?" he asks, cocking his head to the side. His grip tightens on my wrist and I struggle to free it. I let out a nervous chuckle, thinking he'll let go, but he doesn't.

"Let go of my wrist," I say, shaking it.

His fingers dig into my skin as he steps closer to me. I can smell the onion on his breath, mixed with beer and cigarette smoke. It makes my stomach roll.

"Where do you think you're going? The night's still young."

"Home."

My eyes meet his and I see a flash of something unknown in them that sends a shiver down my spine. My heartbeat thumps in my ears as I realize my initial gut feeling was right. I shouldn't have come on this date.

Jake spins us around so that he has the advantage on me. He shoves my shoulder, slamming me against the wall. My head hits the laminate paneling with a soft thud. He leans down to kiss me and I quickly turn my face so that his lips hit my cheek. He grabs my chin and yanks my face towards him, his lips slamming against mine in a horrible attempt to kiss me.

I struggle to get away from him. No one notices, or chooses to look at us, in the dark corner of the bar.

"Jake, stop," I say as I try to wrestle him off of me. It's to no avail, he's stronger than I am.

The hand that used to hold my wrist now sits on my hip, at the edge of my jeans. I feel him work his fingers under the fabric of my shirt and goosebumps spread across my skin as his fingertips skim over the skin there. His touch makes me want to vomit. I feel dirty and violated.

His grimy hand slides up my ribs and then he is palming my breast, fighting with the cup of my bra. Anger ignites within me and the next thing I know, my palm is meeting his face.

His hand falls out of my shirt at the impact and he staggers backwards, looking as if *he* is the one who should be appalled.

"What the hell was that?" I demand.

"Time for a show," he says, rubbing his cheek. It's turning rosy from my palm.

I start to shove past him as his fingertips ghost my wrist again. I yank it toward my body so he can't grasp it and spin around, fire in my eyes, angry that he would dare try to touch me again.

"I told you," he says, "my father can ruin anyone in this town."

"Is that a threat?" I ask, narrowing my eyes.

Jake shrugs. "Make of it what you will."

"Unlike you," I say, snarling, "I don't need my daddy to fight my battles for me. Go to hell, Jake." I stomp my foot down, and it just so happens to be on top of his foot.

I turn on my heel and head toward the door, angrily shoving it open. Fuming, I barrel past the few men entering the bar and out into the parking lot.

My head is spinning and adrenaline is pulsing through my veins. I'm so angry that I can't see straight. I start heading in the general direction of Beth's house, tears welling in my eyes. I can't believe that Jake thought I would be so easy. My mind is stuck in an endless cycle of degrading thoughts as I walk, so much so that I don't notice the sound of a golf cart creeping up behind me. I turn around and my anger and anxiety dissipate when I see Graham behind the wheel.

"Thea!" he says, and I stop walking. He slows the golf cart down to a stop next to me as he adds, "What are you doing in this part of town?"

I wipe at my tear-streaked face and hiccup before I answer him. His face searches mine.

"Thea," he repeats, his voice softer. "Who did this to you?"

"I had a date," I say, in almost a whisper. I sniffle, snot running out of my nose. I quickly wipe it away with the back of my hand. "And it did not go well."

*Understatement of the year,* I think to myself.

"I'm sorry." He stays quiet for a few moments.

"Wait, what are *you* doing here?" I ask as my head clears a bit.

"My mom needed some things from the general store." He pats the plastic bag sitting next to him on the seat. "Do you need a ride home?"

"I can walk, it's fine." I glance back in the direction of the bar, relieved that Jake didn't come after me.

"I'm not letting you walk," Graham says, "Hop in." He scoots the plastic bag closer to his body and pats the seat before I step aboard.

Once I'm settled, he takes off in the direction of Beth's house. My hair blows in the wind as we ride along in silence. He keeps glancing at me as he drives to make sure I'm okay.

"You look pretty," he says quietly.

"I don't feel pretty," I mutter as I play with the hem of my shirt, a loose thread suddenly becoming the most interesting thing I've ever seen.

"Do you want to talk about it?"

A beat passes before I blurt out, "It was Jake Osborne. He groped me.

I see Graham's grip on the steering wheel tighten and swear I see his jaw twitch at the mention of Jake's name.

"Are you okay?" he asks. "I'll beat his ass."

I shake my head. "It's fine."

"No, Thea, it's really not. He shouldn't get away with this."

"He said, 'my father can ruin anyone in this town,'" I say, using air quotes.

Graham rolls his eyes. "His dad is a good lawyer, I'll give him that."

"I just don't want them to come after me or the diner because I turned him down."

He shakes his head. "They have no reason to."

I nod.

"Seriously, though, are you okay?"

"Yeah, just shaken up a bit. I just wanted him to like me." Really, all I want to do is crawl into bed in the fetal position.

"You know I'd kick his ass for you, right?"

I look at him as he comes to a stop at a stop sign.

"I do now," I say quietly, wondering why he would do that for me.

Graham adds, "You deserve more than just the bare minimum."

We ride in silence the rest of the way. I see the living room lamp on through the window and know Beth is waiting for me. I don't want to tell her about the night. I should have avoided this night entirely.

I meet Graham's eyes as he parks the golf cart in the driveway. I take a shaky breath.

"Thanks, Graham," I say as we sit there. There's so much more that I want to say — to thank him for his friendship and for being my savior tonight but I can't find the right words. My voice gets caught in my throat. He doesn't ask any more questions. He doesn't pry, and for that I'm grateful. I just want to put this night to rest.

"Any time," he says softly.

I feel a lump forming in my throat and know that tears are coming.

"I, uh, better head inside," I say as I hop out of the golf cart.

"See you later."

I nod as I turn away and head up the porch steps. A tear escapes and I quickly wipe it away as I fumble with my keys in the lock and open the door. The golf cart rumbles to life as Graham backs down the driveway. I toss my keys onto the entryway table and kick off my shoes, not bothering to put them in the shoe rack.

"Hey," Aunt Beth says, sticking her head out of the living room. "How was your date?"

I look up at her and her smile instantly fades.

"Thea, what's wrong?" she asks.

I sniffle as I shake my head. "I shouldn't have gone," I mutter. "Raquel tried to warn me and I didn't listen."

"Come here." She reaches for me and I follow her into the living room. She guides me to the couch and we sit down. She tucks her legs underneath her and leans against the back of the couch.

"Tell me everything," she says.

"He picked me up on his motorcycle," I begin. "I tried to get him to just walk, but he was adamant about the motorcycle."

Aunt Beth nods slowly. "And it made you panic," she finishes.

I nod. "But I did it, because I didn't want to cause a scene. Then we go to this tavern. He hits on the waitress the entire time, and barely pays any attention to me. Doesn't even pay for my food." I don't mention the beers.

"Gotta kiss a lot of frogs before you find Prince Charming," Beth says. She rubs my arm soothingly.

"That's the thing," I say as I sniffle. "He tried to kiss me and wouldn't take no for an answer. He pinned me against the wall and groped me."

"Thea," she says as eyes search mine. A tenderness falls over her face as she looks at me. "Honey, I'm so sorry."

"I just," I say, my breath shaky, "feel so stupid. I just wanted him to like me." Hot tears spill down my cheeks as I put my head in my hands.

Aunt Beth scoots closer on the couch and wraps her arms around me as I cry.

"Oh, Thea," she murmurs, "I'm sorry. Sounds like he doesn't deserve to even know you. He's an idiot and don't let him break your confidence. You're a great girl and you deserve someone who treats you like the gold you are."

I don't respond.

"I slapped him when he touched me," I say, pulling away to look at her with tearful eyes. "And then took off. I ran into Graham and he brought me here on his golf cart."

Beth nods. "What did you say his last name is?" she asks after a moment.

I pull away and wipe at my face again. "Osborne."

She stiffens. "Listen to me," she says in all seriousness. "I never want you to see him again."

"You don't have to worry about that," I huff. I don't want to re-live this night.

"Seriously, Thea, Osborne boys are no good for you."

"I just feel..." I trail off as I look around the living room, "used."

"I know," she says. "If Jake is anything like his father, and it sounds like he is, he's an ass and a heartbreaker."

"You know his dad?"

"You could...say that."

"How?" I ask.

Beth smiles weakly. "That," she says as she stands up, "is a story for another time. Now, why don't you go put on your pajamas? I'll make you some tea."

I nod as I stand up and sniffle. Beth always seems to know what I need.

She walks into the kitchen, flipping the light on as I pad down the hall to my room. I quickly change into my favorite pajamas, one of Mom's old long sleeve T-shirts and leggings.

Beth is placing a cup of tea on the table just as I walk back into the kitchen.

"Would you...want to bake with me?" I ask as I pick up the warm cup.

She turns around and a smile slowly spreads across her face.

"I'd like that," she says before reaching into the fridge and pulling out the butter. "What do you want to bake?"

"Teach me how to make your cinnamon roll snickerdoodles," I say, "please."

"Your mom always loved those."

"I know. Makes me feel closer to her."

Beth smiles as she pulls the cinnamon from the cabinet.

I take a sip of the tea and set it back down on the table before joining her at the counter and rolling up my sleeves to get to work. I want to bake out this sadness and frustration, get my hands dirty and feel in control of the situation.

And I never want to see Jake ever again.

# Chapter Six

## Beth

Someone is screaming.

My eyes fly open and I blink a few times as they adjust to the darkness of my room. My heart thumps wildly in my chest. I sit up in bed, unsure that I actually heard anything, until I hear it again.

Tossing my covers off, I swing my legs over the side of the bed and get up. It only takes a few steps to get to my bedroom door and the wooden baseball bat I keep behind it. I open the door quietly and glance down the hallway.

There's a different noise now, something more like a whimper, from the other end of the hallway. I realize it's Thea and not an intruder. Padding down the hallway, I set the baseball bat down at her door. She must be having a nightmare; agony flashes across her face in the pale moonlight that streams in from the windows.

"Thea," I say, as I walk to the bed. The sheets are bunched up beneath her fists as she thrashes. She doesn't hear me.

"Thea," I repeat, a little louder. I sit down on the edge of the bed and brush her hair off of her forehead. She jerks under my touch.

"Thea, wake up," I say, raising my voice. I grab her shoulders and gently shake her. "Wake up, it's okay, you're having a nightmare."

Her eyes fly open and she blinks a few times, confusion dancing across her face for the briefest of moments.

"Hey," I whisper, moving hair away from her face. Her skin is coated in a sheen of sweat. "It's okay," I add, "you're safe. It was just a dream."

She rubs at her eyes. "I'm sorry I woke you up," she says after a moment, covering her face with her hands.

"There's no need to apologize. Do you want to talk about it?"

"I keep having the same nightmare, over and over," she sighs, "it's always the wreck. It never goes away." She sits up and puts her head in her hands for a moment. Her shoulders slump as her hands fall to her lap and fingers begin to fidget.

"I'm sorry," she repeats.

"Thea, seriously, it's okay." I reach for her and pull her closer to me, tucking her head just under my chin as I hug her.

"I'm here for you," I murmur as I run my fingers over her hair.

She nods. "How are you so strong?"

"I have my moments," I whisper, tears forming in my eyes as I think about my sister. "Trust me." I feel a tear slide down my face and I wipe at it. "She loved you so very much," I add, my voice not above a whisper. "And I do, too. Together, we'll get through this."

"Some days it doesn't feel like it. Some days it feels like this is all I'll ever be."

"I know. I'm sorry you have to go through this so young."

Thea pulls away from me and searches my eyes. "I'm really glad I came out here," she says quietly after a moment. "I'm glad I have you."

"I am, too." I smile. "You're keeping me young."

This elicits a laugh out of her and I watch her relax a little.

"Really, though," I say, "you're not alone in this."

She nods and yawns.

"Go back to sleep," I murmur as I stand up.

"I never could back in Seattle," she says. "I'd be up for the rest of the night whenever I had one. So...thank you, for comforting me."

"No thanks needed. That's what I'm here for."

Thea settles back against her pillows and I pull the comforter up around her neck. I press a kiss to her forehead.

"We can talk more about this in the morning," I say as I reach the doorframe.

She nods against her pillow. I quietly walk down the hallway, the floor creaking under my feet as I go. I sigh and run my hands through my hair as I close my bedroom door. I hear the click of the doorknob and glance out my window for a moment before I sit down on the edge of my bed, reaching for my phone. I unlock it and shoot off a quick text to Charlie asking if he's still awake.

He calls in an instant.

"Is everything okay?" he asks. "Are you okay? Thea?"

I sigh as I crawl under the covers and lean against my headboard.

"I don't know," I admit. I rub my face with my left hand. "I'm worried about Thea. She's not acting right."

"What do you mean?" Charlie's voice is low and laced with sleep.

"She's been having nightmares about the wreck, she had a date with..." I pause, "a jackass kid... She's not making good decisions."

"She's twenty," Charlie says. "She's going to make some dumbass decisions. We sure as hell did at that age."

"Yeah, but this isn't like her. This seems different. She's got a good head on her shoulders, but she's not acting like it."

He sighs softly. "She also just lost her mom and uprooted her entire life, Beth Ann."

"I don't need logic right now, I just need you to listen to me."

I can hear him smile through the phone. "Okay, Miss Bossy."

"I am not bossy."

"Sure," Charlie says, drawing the word out in a playful manner.

A smile teases its way out of the corner of my lips. "I just don't know how to help her," I admit. "I can't bake my way out of this one."

"As long as she's got you, she'll be okay. You think she'd see a therapist? That might be a good place to start." I hear his bed creak.

"I don't know. Maybe." I glance back out my window. "I just feel helpless."

"I know." I hear him sigh. "But you're not. You've got me."

"Thank God," I say as I transfer my phone to my other hand. "I don't know what I'd do without you."

A comfortable silence settles over us for a few moments and I listen to Charlie's rhythmic breathing.

"I really miss her," I say quietly.

"I know," he repeats, "but I'm sure she's happy knowing that Thea has you."

I stare out the window as tears form in my eyes as I think about my sister. "There's no guidebook for this."

"Unfortunately, no, there's not."

"I feel like I can't let Thea see me break down, because then she'll get upset, and I'm trying my hardest, but it's not easy."

"Maybe that's what she needs, Beth Ann," Charlie says. "Maybe she needs to see that you're human, too, and you miss Caroline just as much as she does. Even Wonder Woman breaks, after all."

At his words, the dam inside me crumbles, releasing the full force of my grief and tears all over again.

"Every time she laughs, I see Caroline in her. Her smile, her spirit. It's just not fair, you know."

"I know." Charlie's voice is comforting and that makes me cry harder. "The good ones go young," he adds.

I clamp my free hand over my mouth to stifle my cries as I sit there on the phone with him.

"Is there anything I can do to help?" he asks.

I don't respond for a few moments. "No," I sigh, a mess of tears and snot. I wipe at my tear-soaked face and sniffle.

"I wish there were," Charlie mutters, "I hate seeing you upset. But at least you and Thea have each other and you're going to get through this together."

He doesn't realize that he's been the life raft in my grief.

I hear him yawn and suddenly, I remember that it's past two in the morning.

"Sorry," I mutter, "you need to sleep instead of listening to me blubber on and on."

"Beth Ann," he warns, "you should know by now that it doesn't matter what time it is. I'm always here for you."

"Thanks," I whisper, feeling another wave of sadness wash over me.

"You sure you're okay?"

"Yeah."

"I don't believe you."

A small chuckle escapes my lips. He's good, he's always been good.

"I will be," I sigh.

He seems content with that answer. "Okay." He pauses. "Good night, Beth Ann. I'll see you at the diner."

"'Night, Charlie," I whisper.

With that, the phone disconnects. I toss it aside on my bed and close my eyes. Memories of Caroline dance through my brain and

God, what I would give for one more day with her. Tears seep out of my eyes and I ball my fists up. I let myself have a few moments to wallow in my grief before I open my eyes again, knowing what I need to do.

I swing my legs back over the side of my bed and reach for the doorknob. I head to the kitchen and flip the light on. Once my eyes have adjusted to the lighting, I grab a dishrag from the counter and run it under the tap. I bring it to my face; the cold is a shock to my system. I toss it aside and then wash my hands before grabbing a mixing bowl from the dish drainer. I reach into the cabinet and pull out the jar of cinnamon before getting the eggs and butter from the fridge.

Caroline always loved my cinnamon roll snickerdoodles, and for tonight, I can pretend I'm making them for her. I close my eyes and envision Caroline standing in my kitchen, us laughing about some stupid, sarcastic remark she made.

I set the ingredients on the counter and get to work.

I check in on Thea before I leave for the morning. She's sleeping peacefully and I don't want to disturb her, even though I do want to talk to her. I figure we can talk once I'm home later in the evening.

It's a peaceful morning in the diner, one I'm glad for since I never went back to sleep after my phone call with Charlie. My eyes feel swollen from crying so much; no amount of eye cream would fix this mess this morning.

I hear the bell above the door ring and glance in its direction, a Pavlovian response after all these years. I watch as a tall, skinny man with short, jet black hair walks through the doors and glances around disapprovingly. He's a man I never thought would walk into my diner ever again.

He spots me and saunters over.

"Beth," he says cordially as he sets his briefcase down on my counter. He pretends to flick lint off of his gray suit.

"James," I say, iciness lacing my voice.

"I'm looking for Thea Calloway," he says, looking around again, a disparaging look on his face.

"Why? That's my niece." I cross my arms over my chest.

He looks at me now as he adjusts his tie awkwardly. "Peculiar," he muses, a sly smile creeping along his face. "I should have known."

I narrow my eyes at him. "What are you talking about?"

We haven't seen each other in years. Granted, Driftbay is small, but I know how to avoid someone if I really want to. And James... I would be content if I never saw him again for the rest of my life.

"You Calloway women sure are kryptonite for Osborne men."

The blood in my veins begins to boil as I stare at him across the counter. Sure, it's been twenty years since he broke my heart, but some wounds you never fully get over.

We were together for six years. I was completely enchanted and when I thought a ring was going to appear, I was informed that our relationship wasn't the fairytale I'd envisioned. I'd been cheated on for half of our relationship. It completely blindsided me.

I thought he was the love of my life, though he never truly respected my dreams. But the sex was good, so I stayed. Charlie and Caroline hated him. Looking back, I realize I was settling. He tore my self esteem to shreds but I still looked at him with stars in my eyes. It took a lot of therapy sessions to bounce back from that breakup.

I stare at him as he adjusts the burgundy tie around his neck again with long, slender fingers.

"Thea," he begins, "it seems, put her hands on my son."

"She didn't start things, but she sure as hell ended them," I say, snapping out of the past. "I believe your son is the one who put his hands on her first and wouldn't take the word no for an answer."

James leans across the counter and lowers his voice. "If she ever touches him again, there will be charges pressed."

"You don't have to worry about that," I say, "because she's never going to see your scum of a son ever again." I uncross my arms now, rage pulsating through my body.

"Be careful how you speak of my son." James glares at me.

"Or what, James?" I retort. I don't give him a chance to response as my fists ball at my sides. "Get out of my diner," I add, doing my best to keep my tone even.

He smirks at me, and turns to go.

"Always a pleasure, Beth," he says, the words sliding off his tongue like liquor.

I stretch my neck after he's gone, feeling the anger radiating through my body and tension taking root. I take a deep breath to calm down. I don't know what I ever saw in him.

Penny catches my gaze from across the diner, having caught the end of my interaction with James.

"I need a minute," I tell her as she crosses behind the counter.

"Okay," she says, nodding with wide eyes. She's never seen me lose my cool before.

I march off to my office and slam the door behind me. It shocks me that even after all this time, James can still elicit this kind of reaction from me. I lean against the door and close my eyes, focusing on steadying my breathing.

*Five things you can see,* I think, reverting back to my therapy days.

I glance around my office, focusing on the gigantic calculator on my desk, the jar of pens, my notepad, the stapler, and the calendar hanging above the wall. I take another breath in.

*Four things you can touch.*

My fingertips graze the hem of my T-shirt. I run my right hand over the door behind me, before I walk towards my desk. I sit down in my chair and slide my hand over the leather armrest and then play with the cap of the discarded highlighter on my desk.

*Three things you can hear.*

I close my eyes and focus on my breathing, in and out. I can hear music through the wall coming from the kitchen, but I can't make out the lyrics. I can also hear the hum of the air-conditioner. It's methodical, enough to lull me to sleep.

*Two things you can smell.*

There's the air freshener I'd plugged in a while ago, some artificial Hawaiian breeze scent I'd picked up at the general store. I catch a whiff of my perfume as I reach for the packet of gum across the desk, the one thing I can taste.

I pop a piece into my mouth, my senses temporarily overwhelmed with the flavor of wintergreen gum.

I feel centered again, but take a few extra moments before returning to the roaring life of the diner.

By the time I reach the counter again, Charlie is at his usual barstool.

"Hey," he says, smiling as he spots me.

He looks at me and my bad mood starts to melt.

"Hi," I say as I pop my gum.

"You okay?" he asks. Whether it's because we've been friends for so long or because he's a cop, he can read me like a book.

"James came in." I lean against the counter and cross my arms.

"What the hell did he want?" Charlie's happy mood vanishes in an instant.

"Apparently, that date Thea went on was with his son." I push off the counter and turn around to grab a mug for his coffee.

"Seriously?" he asks.

I nod as I grab the coffee pot and pour it into his mug. "I didn't ask enough questions when she told me about it. Had I known it was with Jake Osborne, I wouldn't have let her go," I say over my shoulder.

"It's not your fault, Beth Ann," he says as I turn back to him and hand him his mug.

"I know, but maybe I could have protected her more. Saved another Calloway woman from the curse of the Osbornes."

Charlie chokes on his coffee, stifling a laugh. I see a grin on his face over the top of his mug.

"I don't know what you ever saw in him," he mutters.

"Truthfully, I don't either," I say, as I lean back against the counter. James was nice enough in the beginning and I guess that's what hooked me. It wasn't until we were deep into our relationship that things started changing between us and he became someone I no longer recognized.

"Caroline would kill me if she knew I let her daughter go out with his son," I mutter.

Charlie cocks his head to the side. "We did have that mutual hatred in common." He searches my face. "Did you go back to sleep after our phone call? You look tired."

"Thanks," I laugh, "for telling me I look like shit."

He backpedals now. "I didn't mean it like that."

"I know." I grin now. "Just giving you hell. But the answer is no, I didn't. Baked instead." I walk over to the side of the counter and grab the display plate before walking back over to him.

"Cinnamon roll snickerdoodles, Caroline's favorite," I say, setting the plate down in front of him.

Charlie surveys the cookies carefully before selecting one. He takes a bite and nods. "Caroline had good taste." He swallows and then asks, "Did you talk to Thea about therapy?"

"No," I sigh, "she was still asleep when I left and I didn't want to disturb her."

"Have *you* thought about it? It might be good for you both. What about that therapist you used to see?"

"She doesn't practice anymore." Part of my hesitation about going back to therapy is that I would have to start back at square one. It took me long enough to find one when I was dealing with heartbreak from James.

"Could be worth pursuing," Charlie says. "I just want the best for you both."

It's as if time inside the restaurant slows down. The knot in my stomach transforms into butterflies. I so desperately want to tell him how I truly feel.

I take a shaky breath and feel the words barreling to the surface, ready to tumble over my tongue. I open my mouth just as a loud crash echoes through the diner. Penny stands in front of an occupied booth, a tray of food splattered across the floor at her feet. The woman in the booth starts apologizing profusely as she pulls her toddler into the seat. The diner springs back to real-time around me and I rush over to help, feelings of Charlie momentarily forgotten.

# Chapter Seven

## Thea

Beth is still in bed, but I'm too excited to sleep. Today is my first official day at Beth Ann's Diner and I've been buzzing with anticipation all night. Streetlamps guide part of my way as I begin my usual trek to the diner, my arms full of a tray of cookies and a lemon pie I'd made when I was too amped up to sleep. The sun is rising as I arrive at the diner. The sky is painted in bright, beautiful opalite colors, and the new recipe I've been wanting to try — blueberry lemon scones — is gnawing at the back of my mind.

I carefully walk up the steps to the back porch, balancing the desserts in my arms. Beth gave me a key the night before and I fumble with it as I try to unlock the door.

The kitchen comes to life before me and I feel my heart swell with excitement as I look around. It's the kitchen of my dreams. I can bake multiple treats at once with the dual ovens and every utensil under the sun is at my disposal. I see all of the possibilities as I stare at the space, letting myself wonder what this could lead to, just for a moment. Lately, I've toyed with the idea of opening up my own bakery but it seems a bit...unambitious when my mom was a neurosurgeon.

I close the door behind me and then familiarize myself with the kitchen, learning what hides behind cabinet doors and what lives in the drawers. I find some display plates in a cabinet and place the cookies on one, leaving them on the counter so I remember to take it up front before we open. I put the pie in one of the refrigerators and then check out the back room. There're a few tables and scattered chairs, a bulletin board with this week's schedule, another refrigerator, and a counter with a small television and microwave. I see a tower of lockers on one side of the room and pick one without a lock, tossing my phone, keys, and wallet inside. I walk back into the kitchen and roll up my sleeves, grabbing a black apron from the hook by the door. I tie it around my waist and after a little trial and error, gather all of the ingredients needed for my recipe and get to work.

I can hear Beth in her office preparing the daily deposit as I crack an egg into a large metal bowl. She arrived not long after me and has been pecking at the monstrous accounting calculator on her desk ever since. She should really give up more control of the diner, but I understand her reservations in doing so. I hum a song to drown her out and begin to whisk flour into the eggs in the bowl. I become lost in my own little world of sugar, butter, and flour when I hear the back door open again.

I glance over my shoulder and see Graham in the doorway, illuminated in the early morning rays of sunlight. It glistens off his sandy-colored hair, making him look like a Greek god.

He smiles as he walks toward me.

"Well, well, well," he says, peering over my shoulder at what I'm making. "What do we have here?"

"The beginning of blueberry lemon scones, if all goes according to plan," I say as I add more flour, "or recipe, I should say."

He laughs. "I can't wait to try one."

I grin as I look over my shoulder.

Graham ducks into the backroom and I hear him toss his belongings into a locker.

"What are you doing here so early?" I ask when he returns to the kitchen.

He nods toward the cart of fresh silverware and clean napkins in the corner. "They aren't going to roll themselves."

"Isn't that a bit below your pay grade?" I ask as I watch him roll the cart over to the counter in front of me. He drags a barstool across the floor and sits. I assumed a busboy would have done it last night, but now that I think about it, I haven't noticed one around the diner. Of course, I've only met a handful of Beth's employees.

He shrugs and starts rolling a set, making quick work of it. "I do whatever Beth asks of me," he says simply.

I ponder what he's said for a moment, until a specific memory pops into my head. "Including bringing a surfboard in here?"

He laughs and the sound of it wraps around me like honey — sticky, sweet, and golden. It's a sound I could get used to hearing for the rest of my life.

Graham smiles at the memory. "Sometimes I just like to give her crap." He finishes a utensil set and places it back on the cart.

It's my turn to laugh now. I picture his mischievous grin and my heart does a somersault.

"Besides," he says, gesturing at the mound of silver in front of him, "she's been good to me."

"How so?" I prompt. I hope it's not too invasive. While I've known him nearly as long as I've been in Driftbay, I want to learn more about him and his relationship with Beth. Happy with the mixture in my bowl, I turn it over and dump the dough out onto the counter. I reach for more flour and sprinkle it around the dough.

Graham nods. "I've worked here since I was fifteen. She took a chance on me when I was just a kid." He shakes his head at the memories. "She's seen me through some of the worst times in my life."

Ah. We have that in common.

I stay quiet, hoping he'll continue.

"I started as a busboy and did some prep work on the weekends while I was still in high school. I worked as much as I could. Got promoted to waiter once I hit eighteen and graduated. I practically lived here that summer, trying to make as much money as I could for college. Then, I went to the university a couple of towns over and worked on the weekends doing whatever she needed." He pauses before continuing, "I loaded up on credit hours my first couple of semesters so I could graduate a year early. I got my bachelor's in computer science."

"Yet you're still here." I stare at him with my head cocked to the side, letting my hands rest in the dough in front of me.

"Yeah," he sighs, "my original plan was to move to a big city and get away from Driftbay once I got my degree, but life got in the way." He keeps rolling silverware as I grab a baking sheet from across the kitchen for my scones.

"Life has a way of doing that," I say, sighing as I think about how life got in my way. I set the baking sheet down beside my mound of dough and grab a knife to start cutting it into triangle-shaped pieces.

"My parents divorced during my senior year of college and then my mom got sick. So leaving...wasn't exactly an option," he explains.

I transfer a scone to the baking sheet. "I'm sorry," I say, keeping my voice soft.

He shrugs. "Apparently, my dad had wanted to leave for a while, but waited until the beginning of my senior year. I was already locked into my college classes. I wanted to leave, but I couldn't. At that point, I would have had to pay back my scholarship and I couldn't afford to do that."

"Wow. I'm really sorry."

"It hit me hard, it was a nasty divorce. I'm not sure how I managed to pass that semester. I completely fell apart. Truthfully, I think my professors just felt sorry for me. I went from being a straight-A student to barely passing."

"You know the old saying," I say as I wipe at my brow, "'C's get degrees.'"

Graham nods. "Yeah, but I worked hard for my grades. I earned a high achiever's scholarship that covered the majority of my tuition and books. It really helped my family out. I was the third kid in the family to go to college, so my parents were stressed about money."

I can relate to that. Mom pushed me to do well in school, just like Graham's parents obviously had. She had always talked about scholarships and setting myself up for success down the road. Her game plan was three steps ahead.

He continues. "I knew he obviously wasn't happy if he'd been wanting to leave, but to end a twenty-year marriage like it's nothing? And at the same time, what about me? I was just finding my footing as an adult. He derailed my life trying to change his. I almost flunked out, almost lost my scholarship. I know I can't blame it all on my parents, but it really affected me. It was like my worst childhood fear come to life."

He starts rolling the silverware more aggressively.

I can't imagine the pain he must have felt watching his family be ripped apart by his father. I can, however, relate to the pain he felt watching his entire world crumble beneath him.

"I get it," I say quietly, cutting more dough. "Trust me, I get it." I place the last few on the baking sheet.

"I'm sorry that you do."

We work in silence for a few moments, the air as thick as the dough between my hands.

"I have two older sisters," he begins again, "but they have their own lives and families, so I was the only one still at home when it happened. Ginny, the oldest, is a teacher in Boston. She's got two daughters, Melody and Cosette. I don't get to see them as often as I'd like."

"That can't be easy," I say.

He shakes his head. "Betty is in the medical field and just moved to Chicago a couple of years ago. They were as supportive as they could be, but it's not the same as if they were here, in the thick of it."

I understand what he means. People tried to be there for me when my mom died, but it felt like I was lost at sea and they were just waving at me from the shore, telling me to swim.

"It must be nice, though, having siblings," I say. "I'm an only child so I can't relate."

"You know," he says, leaning back on the stool as he works. "Growing up, I always wished I was an only child and thought my sisters were so annoying."

I laugh. "Don't all little brothers think that?"

Graham smiles and picks up more silverware. "Now, I'm grateful for them. I haven't spoken to my father in years. It broke something in me when he left, and I just never got over it. I don't know that I ever will."

"Graham," I say, "That's a lot."

"Sorry," he shrugs. "I didn't mean to dump all of that on you."

I look up at him and for the first time, really look at him. I see a frightened little boy in man's clothing, a child just aching for their parent. He wears his melancholy comfortably, hiding it the best he can behind a smile. Still, sadness lurks beyond his eyes. I can see the broken pieces, the jagged edges spewing every way, creating a fence around his heart to avoid any further hurt. Mostly, what I see is someone just wanting love.

"He moved a couple of towns over, the last I knew. My sisters still talk to him. He's tried to get in contact with me a few times but I just can't talk to him. Seeing how much pain he put my mom through..." he trails off.

"Not to mention all of the pain he put *you* through." I grab the baking tray and walk over to the oven, opening it. The hot air rushes out and blasts me in the face as I shove the tray in. I close the door and walk back to the counter, waiting for Graham to meet my eyes. "Hurting your spouse is one thing, but hurting your child is a different kind of low."

He nods in agreement, as if to say I've made an excellent point. "And then, Mom got sick."

I grab the timer I'd found earlier and set it, raising my eyebrows to urge him to continue.

"Severe spinal stenosis. Her spine was compressing a nerve that ran through her left leg. Her leg would go numb and just give out. It was so bad that she was falling all of the time, just at the drop of a dime. She was losing motor function rapidly. We thought she'd end up in a wheelchair before we finally found a doctor that would help her and do surgery."

A pain goes through my heart at his words. My mom would have helped in any way she could in a situation like that. That's the kind of person, and doctor, she was.

"So then, she had surgery and extensive physical therapy. I was there for all of it. I mean, I was the *only* one there for all of it. Ginny and Betty flew in for her surgery and stayed a few days after with us, but I was the one taking her to appointments and getting her to physical therapy and all of that."

"That's a lot on you," I say, "to be the caretaker like that." I search for another baking sheet so I can cut out more scones to bake.

"I didn't mind," he says. "I mean, she's my mom and I would do anything for her. But part of me resents my father for leaving because of that. I wanted to move away from Driftbay and experience the world, but once he left, I felt like I didn't have a choice. I had this gut feeling that I needed to stay here for her, and it turned out I was right."

"You have to follow your heart," I tell him as I walk back to the counter. "Your heart wants what it wants," I add, thinking of Judith. "Besides, maybe there's some other reason you were meant to stay in Driftbay."

"I guess you're right." Graham frowns as he rolls another packet of silverware. "I guess you could say the same thing about my dad. He followed what his heart wanted in the end."

I bite the inside of my cheek as I consider his words, having played devil's advocate. I shrug as he sighs.

"They were just...supposed to grow old together, you know? In sickness and in health and whatnot."

The words hang in the air as I begin cutting out my second tray of scones.

"So, what about you?" he asks. "I've bared my soul to you. What's your tragic backstory?"

I laugh, wiping my flour-covered hands on my apron. I take a breath before I begin. "Well, I lived in Seattle before I moved here, as you know."

He nods.

"Born and raised there. My mother was a neurosurgeon. One of the best in the country. She uh," I pause, taking a deep breath, "...died in a car accident in January."

"Wow, Thea," Graham mumbles. "I'm sorry. I was just joking about the tragic backstory."

I laugh half-heartedly and continue. "I don't have any siblings. It was just my mom and I growing up. And Aunt Beth, of course, though we didn't get out here to see her as much as we wanted to." Memories of those few beach vacations flood my mind, the days of yesteryear filled with sandy shorelines, salty air, and sweet hugs.

"I don't know who my dad is. Mom really wanted a kid and didn't have the time, or the patience, to search for Mr. Right. So, instead she used a sperm donor and chose my biological father from a catalog of superior genetic specimens. She was searching for the best of the best." I smile weakly at Graham, knowing I am anything but the best of the best.

"When I was younger, I'd get so mad at her for making me grow up without a dad."

He stands and stretches as I grab another bowl and start to whisk together ingredients for my lemon glaze.

"They're not all they're cracked up to be," he says. "Don't get me wrong, my dad was great when I was growing up. His recent actions just really tarnished all the good years for me."

I nod. "I didn't really have a lot of friends growing up. I met my best friend at my first job. God, we hated working there. Our boss was crazy." I laugh to myself as memories replay in my head.

I recount how my former boss would throw hangers across the stockroom when she was angry and Graham chuckles.

"I was your typical high school student. Made solid B's. I could have made better grades if I'd just applied myself more. Instead, I'm just average." I shrug, the lemony, citrus scent of the glaze working its way to my nose.

He stops what he's doing, his fingers frozen on a fork.

"You are anything but average, Thea," he says.

We stare at each other, our breathing the only sound in the kitchen.

"Never played sports," I say, clearing my throat. "Not coordinated enough for that. I did a couple of semesters at a community college, trying to figure out what I wanted to do with my life. People expect greatness from me, being Dr. Calloway's daughter."

"I imagine that's hard, living in her shadow." Graham's fingers make light work of the utensils now.

"At times, yes. Here in Driftbay, though...no one knows her. Well, except for Beth. It's...almost a relief." I set the mixing bowl to the side, content with the consistency of the glaze I've concocted.

"I left school after the accident. I just couldn't continue."

"I'm sorry. I know how hard it is," he says softly.

"I was in the car with her that night. Really, it's my fault we were even out." Memories of that fateful night flood my memory and I feel my pulse quicken, even though I know I'm safe here with Graham. I can talk about this. "I'd begged her to go out shopping, though the forecast was calling for a bad snowstorm later that night. She died and I walked away unscathed. Sometimes I feel guilty for making it out alive. She saved so many lives. Cars still freak me out." I blink my eyes rapidly, fighting the tears that are surfacing. "She gave people hope when they had none and gave them their lives back. I just... bake."

I reach up to brush the tears with one hand.

"Hey," Graham says gently, walking around the counter. He grips my forearms and turns me to face him. "It's okay. Listen to me. You are not responsible for your mother's death, Thea." His eyes search mine. "You survived for a reason, even if it is 'just baking.' Personally, I think your cookies are life-changing."

I let out a laugh, breaking up the seriousness of the moment. I drink in the feel of him being this close to me, the feel of his hands on me. The sensation makes me shiver. I can smell his cologne; it's woodsy, outdoorsy and I can detect a hint of vanilla in it. It mixes beautifully with the blueberry aroma wafting up from the oven now that the scones are baking. The scents wrap around me, almost suffocating me. It feels like I'm getting drunk on him alone.

"You've got something right here," he whispers as he reaches for my face. The pad of his thumb gently brushes my cheek as he wipes flour off of me.

Our eyes lock on each other and for a moment, I think I know what's going to happen next. I can sense the monumental shift between us as he starts to move closer, as he cradles my head in his large hands, and as my butterflies take flight.

I should be stopping this, especially after my not-so-great date with Jake, but Graham is making me feel things Jake never could.

We're interrupted by a flurry of activity in the doorway. We jump, breaking apart as Beth appears with a handful of papers, her morning till counts.

"Good morning," she says as she narrows her eyes, looking between us. "Am I interrupting something?" she asks, motioning with the papers in her hand.

"No," Graham and I answer in unison. He clears his throat and walks back around the other counter as I reach for my second baking tray. I hastily walk over to the oven and open it. A gush of hot blueberry-scented air escapes. I stick the other tray in and close the door as Graham starts wheeling the cart of silverware to the front of the diner.

I feel Beth's gaze on me and my cheeks start to burn. Whether it's the embarrassment or the oven air, I'm not sure.

She doesn't say another word. Her eyes linger on me for a moment before she turns on her heels and is gone, forgetting what she'd come into the kitchen for.

I'm left alone. I'm flushed and to be quite honest, a bit flustered. I blow a strand of hair out of my face from the corner of my mouth and can't help but wonder what the hell just happened.

# Chapter Eight

## Beth

Hiring Thea was a good business move. It's been several weeks now and word has spread throughout Driftbay about my surprise new baker. Some folks are treating us more as a bakery than a diner, coming in just for Thea's treats. It's strange, really, but I'll take the business.

Thea seems happier now that she's settled into a routine. Part-time quickly evolved into full-time and she seems to really enjoy the early mornings in the kitchen. She's even started concocting her own original recipes, and dare I say it...she might actually be better than me in the baking department.

We did not adequately prepare for the amount of people interested in trying her creations during the first week. Word spread quickly and now she makes a variety of confections each morning, which keeps her busy for hours.

Ever since I caught her and Graham in their almost-kiss in the kitchen, she's been jumpy and almost avoiding me. Well, as much as you can avoid someone when you live and work together. We haven't talked about it, as much as I want to. She deserves some happiness after so much sorrow this year, but I don't know if she's ready to jump into a relationship. Graham is a sweet enough kid, especially after her disastrous date with Jake.

Graham is off this morning and Brian is running the kitchen with Thea. Raquel and another waitress are taking orders and bussing tables like the superstars they are. It's relatively quiet for a Monday morning, something I'll gladly take after the whirlwind weekend.

I'm at my post behind the counter, taking a moment to observe the diner. I'm proud of what I've built in here with these people. They can always handle whatever is thrown at them — be it lines out the door and wrapped around the building, rowdy crowds, or supply chain issues. I've got a good group of people around me and I know the diner wouldn't be what it is without them. I glance approvingly at the wall of awards we've won — best breakfast restaurant in Driftbay for thirteen years running.

I'm wiping down menus and restocking napkin dispensers when Charlie walks in, right on schedule.

"Morning," I say, in a cheerful tone as he sits down on his usual barstool in front of me.

"Good morning," he says. He avoids my eyes as he picks up a menu from the pile I've wiped down. The lack of calling me 'Beth Ann' has me concerned.

"In the mood to try something new?" I tease him. Charlie has had the same breakfast order — scrambled eggs and two pieces of bacon — for years now.

He places the menu back down in the pile on the counter. "I have news," he says, a bit nervously.

"I love news," I say. I toss the dish towel over my right shoulder, lean against the counter, and give him my full attention. After thirty-five years, I know him well enough to know this must be something good.

"I'm," he begins, "going on a date." He chuckles a little as he says the words, relaxing some. "And I feel like a teenager again saying that."

I struggle to keep a smile plastered on my face. It feels like someone just punched me in the gut, leaving me breathless and gasping for air.

"Oh!" It comes out an octave higher than I intended and I know he'll notice.

"Beth Ann," he says, looking concerned.

"No, this is good!" I reach for the dish towel on my shoulder. "This is good," I repeat. "I mean, we've talked about this. We're both free to see other people, we're just friends." I smile. "This is great. Tell me more."

He narrows his eyes as he looks at me, watching for any slight betrayal of my body language before he continues. "I met her online. She sent me a message, we started talking, and it seems like we just really click."

"Oh my God, you aren't on one of those ridiculous dating apps, are you?" I ask as I push off the counter. I grab a mug and fill it with coffee before setting it in front of him.

Charlie suppresses a grin. "Maybe," he says.

I roll my eyes and laugh.

"Are you sure you're okay with it?" he asks.

"Of course," I say. "You don't need to ask my permission to go on a date. You're going, you told me, and we're talking about it. Everything's fine."

"Have I ever told you what a good friend you are?" He smiles that boyish grin of his that makes me weak in the knees and I lean against the counter again for stability.

"You've mentioned it once or twice," I say, a playful smirk tugging at the corners of my mouth.

Charlie visibly relaxes and I know I have him fooled.

*Give me an Academy Award for my performance*, I think to myself.

"Did you come here just for that or did you want breakfast, too?" I ask him.

"Little bit of both."

"Okay," I say, scooting the menus over. I call out to Brian in the kitchen and remind him that Charlie is here. I turn back to face him, folding my arms against my chest and resting them on the countertop. "Tell me everything."

"Her name is Sara," he starts as he wraps his hands around the mug, "She's a high school math teacher here in town."

*I don't have time for a relationship,* I remind myself. I have the diner and that's enough for me.

*But the diner doesn't keep you warm at night,* another voice whispers.

He tells me how they matched on Flyrt — a popular dating app that I'm surprised he even knows the name of. I wouldn't peg Charlie for the dating app kind of guy. Sara sent him a message and they just started chatting — talking about any and everything under the sun, starting to find more in common than they realized.

Brian slides a plate through the kitchen window and rings the bell, getting my attention. I turn and reach for it before setting it down in front of Charlie. He continues to tell me that he plans to take Sara to Regiano's, the Italian restaurant in town. I've been there a few times and have to admit, it's a good atmosphere for a first date.

"Have you thought about what you'll wear?" I ask him, knowing he hasn't.

"Not in the slightest," he laughs, choking on a forkful of eggs.

"This is important, you only get one first impression. Wear that gray button down of yours."

It's my favorite — it makes his dark blue eyes pop. It brings out the gray undertone in them, and reminds me of the sea at dusk — dark, ferocious, and all-consuming.

He nods. "Noted." He stares at me intently as he eats. "Are you really sure you're okay with this?"

I smile again, feeling like the Cheshire Cat. "Yes," I say, lying through my teeth. Besides, saying no wouldn't change the fact that he's going on a date. All it would do is cause a rift between us and I couldn't bear to lose my best friend.

"I'm looking forward to it," he says. "It's been a long time since I got back out there."

I stare at him as he takes another bite of his breakfast. He's right, it has been a while for him. He's had a few sporadic dates off and on over the years, but nothing stuck.

I, on the other hand, swore off dating after my relationship with James went up in flames and that was twenty years ago.

Charlie finishes his food and we go about our daily routine. He pays and leaves shortly after. There's an extra pep in his step, a swagger I hadn't noticed before. I laugh as I watch him exit the diner before my smile fades and reality sets in. My heart feels heavy and I just want to go home, but I have a long afternoon in front of me.

No day is complete without a visit from Judith. I hear the bell above the door chime as she walks in, not long after Charlie left.

"Morning, dearie," she calls, as she heads toward her usual booth.

"Morning, Judith!" I grab a glass from the counter and fill it with ice water before I meet her at her usual table. I pull a straw out of the pocket of my apron and set them both down.

"What's wrong?" she asks, instantly sensing that something is off.

"Nothing." I muster a smile as I grab my notepad to take her order.

"Cut the crap," she says bluntly, and motions to the open side of her booth. "Sit." She unwraps her straw and dunks it into her ice water as she stares at me.

I relent, shoving my notepad and pen back into my apron. I slide into the booth and begin fidgeting with the discarded straw wrapper, staying quiet.

Her hands reach across the table and cover mine, stopping my anxious fidgeting. They're a bit cold this morning and I find myself staring at the wrinkles covering them to avoid meeting her gaze.

"Something's wrong with you. Don't lie to me, please."

I sigh. "I'm just..." I let myself trail off as I look around the diner, refusing to meet her eyes. "I don't know if I'm supposed to tell you this. It's not exactly my story to tell," I admit.

"I won't tell a soul." Judith mimes zipping her lips and then the floor is all mine.

"Charlie told me he has a date."

There. I said it. It's out in the open now. I let out a sigh of relief having gotten it off my chest.

"And you feel...?" she motions at me to continue.

"I don't know." It's an honest answer. I'm confused by my reaction. The logical side of me is happy for Charlie. He deserves to find someone that makes him happy. But the emotional side...well, is pretty damn sad. I've been aware that I have feelings for him for a while now. I thought I had convinced myself into believing that having him as a friend would be enough.

"Confused," Judith finishes. She cocks her head to the side as she stares at me, reading me like a book. "Angry. Sad."

I nod. She's right, like always.

"I just didn't think I would feel this conflicted about it," I admit.

"Matters of the heart are never simple, dearie."

"How are you so wise?" I ask as I look at her, seeing the wealth of wisdom — the kind you only get as you age — on her face.

"Oh, I'm not *so* wise, dearie." She pats my hands. "I've just learned to go after what I want and not give a damn. Now," she says as she shifts in the booth, her bracelets jangling, "what are you going to do about it?"

I shrug. "I don't know. I mean, what can I really do?"

"You could tell Charlie how you feel, for one."

*And potentially ruin our friendship? I think not.*

"Besides that?" I ask, hoping she has another suggestion in her bag of tricks.

"Really, there's nothing else beside that. Either you tell him how you feel or you live like this," she waves her hand at me, "in limbo and be confused and angry all the time. And that is not good for your skin, I might add."

It draws a laugh out of me. Leave it to Judith to always be able to make me laugh.

"Remember what I told you?" she asks, sounding like my mother.

"Yes," I say, somewhat begrudgingly.

I'm beginning to think that Judith is somewhat of a guardian angel. I don't plan to tell Charlie how I feel, but maybe I can learn to live with it. For a moment, I laugh with Judith and there's clarity.

"What did Thea make today?" she asks, craning her neck to see the dessert display case at the front of the diner.

I follow her gaze to see what's left. "Looks like strawberry muffins and cinnamon coffee cake."

She smiles as she turns back to me. "I'll take one of each."

I unlock the door and chuck my shoes off in the entryway, dropping my purse on the floor. Thea is having a girls night with Penny and Raquel, so I have the house to myself. I plan on taking a nice, relaxing bubble bath and maybe diving into a good book, but not before drowning my sorrows in some pizza and vodka. I toss my keys into the dish on the table before walking straight to the fridge for a stiff drink.

One of the things I love about Driftbay is how small it is. Convenience is key. The pizza I ordered before I left the diner should be here any minute. It's from Ramona's Pizzeria, my absolute favorite little pizza place in town. They make their own sauce from a secret recipe handed down through generations and their crust is flaky, buttery, and out of this world. I've eaten it since college and get the same quality food each and every time.

I open the fridge door and immediately reach for the vodka bottle from the back of the top shelf. I cock my head as I stare at it — it doesn't seem as full as I remember. I shake my head, chalking it up to cloudy memory and grab a glass from the cabinet.

The house is quiet as I unscrew the lid and flick it off, thinking about the day. I hear it dance across the linoleum and out of sigh.

*Oh well, I'll find it later,* I think with a shrug. That's a problem for Later Beth.

I pour some vodka into the glass and bring it to my lips. I'm ready to feel that mind-numbing burn, to let this stressful day fade away, at least for a few hours.

Except...there is no burn.

I frown and take another sip. Definitely not vodka. I dump the glass out and bring the bottle to my lips.

It's WATER.

There is only one other person in this house.

I feel anger pulsing through my veins as I stare at the bottle. I grab it and turn it upside down in the sink and watch as the water bubbles out of it. Leaning on the counter, I put my head in my hands.

I'm disappointed. I'm disappointed that I'm out of vodka, when I was so looking forward to a drink, but more importantly, I'm disappointed in Thea. I know I need to address this and get in front of it, but after the day I've had, all I want to do is crawl into bed and have myself a good cry. I don't even want to bake. These feelings are just too big to be folded down into something sugary sweet.

I feel myself sinking down, my feet sliding against the linoleum flooring. I go down, bracing myself against the cabinets. My elbows are propped on my knees and hands locked in my hair. It's the beginning of a breakdown and I welcome it.

I cry.

I'm not one to cry often. If I don't bake, I tend to shove my feelings down until they boil over and I have a meltdown. Tonight, my emotions are ablaze about Charlie and Thea, both of whom I hold dear.

I cry for Thea. I've obviously not done a great job as her guardian or her aunt if she's secretly drinking away her grief. I cry for the pain she must be feeling. I thought she was doing better. I cry for the loss of her mom and my sister. I wish I could call her for advice, but I can't. I cry because of Charlie. I've been pushing my feelings for him aside for nearly three and a half decades. I've been content with him as my best friend because it's safe. I haven't had to worry about getting hurt if things ended badly between us.

The doorbell rings and I glance in its direction as I sniffle. There's no way in hell I'm going to answer it right now. Maybe the delivery boy will just leave my pizza at the door.

I relax my knees and let my legs straighten out. I'm a blubbering mess, crying on my kitchen floor, tear streaks staining my cheeks. I'm sure my mascara is leaving black streaks down my face. My nose is running and I wipe at it with my shirt sleeve.

I want to see Charlie happy. Truly, I do. And if that means sacrificing my own happiness...well, then I guess that's the price I have to pay.

I'm better off alone, anyways. I've always been better off alone. The diner is enough for me.

It has to be.

As for Thea...I don't know what to do. I never intended to be a parent and even though she's legally an adult, she still needs a parental-figure to guide her. She's still a kid.

"Caroline," I whisper, as if the ghost of my sister can hear me, "tell me what I'm supposed to do."

Caroline was the oldest. She always knew what to do. Growing up, any problem I had could be solved by my older sister. She stood up to playground bullies for me, helped me with spelling homework when I struggled, and told me which boys in high school to ignore. She was there for me in a way our parents couldn't be, even into adulthood. She blazed the trail with intensity so I could travel it at my own pace. I sought her opinion on every big decision in my life. And now, making them without her is harder than I ever imagined it would be.

Shakily, I stand up. I let out a sigh and wipe my hands on my jeans. I turn to the sink and quickly wash my hands and splash water on my face. The coldness sends a shock through my system and helps clear my head. I grab a fresh dish towel and dry my hands and face and then toss it back onto the counter.

I reach for the browning bananas on the other side of the counter and then flip the oven into pre-heating mode. Gathering my ingredients from the pantry and refrigerator, I get to work.

I whip up the banana bread mixture, mixing it by hand. I've always preferred to do it by hand; it helps to really work out the emotions I'm feeling. I sniffle as I work, the remnants of my breakdown still lingering. My eyes feel puffy and I make a mental note to use extra eye cream tonight.

Stirring my sadness away, I pour the batter into a baking dish, sprinkle some chocolate chips on top, and stick it into the oven. I set a timer just as I hear a key in the front doorknob and know it must be Thea. I have a clearer head and feel ready to face her.

I grab the bottle from the sink and turn to face the doorway just as she walks in, holding my pizza box.

"Want to explain this?" I ask, holding the empty bottle up.

Thea freezes, the smile fading from her face. She sets the pizza on the table in the corner and starts to look away.

"Look at me," I say. My voice is calm, but icy.

Her eyes fly back to me and we stare at each other for a few moments. She is squirming under my gaze, shuffling uneasily on her feet and biting her lip.

"Um, I..." she stammers and laughs nervously. "You see..."

"Cut the crap, Thea." I set the bottle down on the counter behind me. "There are only two people in this house and I didn't replace the vodka with water."

She looks down at her feet, just like she used to when she was a little girl in trouble with Caroline.

"It was her birthday," she mumbles, "and you left me alone."

"Are you saying this is my fault?" I shoot back.

"No," she says quickly, backpedaling. "I just didn't want to be alone on her birthday and you said you'd be here and I was just *so* sad."

I feel about two feet tall. I'd promised not to leave her alone that day, but two of my waitresses had called out and I couldn't get anyone to cover, and then I'd forgotten entirely with the busyness of my day.

"I'm sorry," she says softly, still looking at her feet. "I just don't know what to do with all the sadness. Baking didn't help."

There's silence for a few moments before I speak.

"*I'm* sorry," I say, stepping closer to her. "I shouldn't have left you alone." I walk over to her and wrap my arms around her. She buries her head in my hair and I feel her start crying. Her body shakes as she lets her grief out. I feel the full weight of what she's been carrying.

"I just miss her," she mumbles. I can barely make it out as she sobs and gasps for air.

"I miss her, too." I gently stroke her hair in an attempt to soothe her. "But you cannot drink your grief away, do you hear me?"

She pulls away as she nods and I reach for her face, gently wiping at the tears staining her cheeks. The scent of banana bread wafts around us like a hug.

As much as I want to lecture her further, I can sense that it's not what she needs at the moment. She needs someone to be there for her, to let her know she's not as alone as she might feel.

"Look," I say, "we've both had a hell of a day. Why don't you eat and take a shower and get some rest? We can talk more about this tomorrow."

Thea nods again and sniffles. "That sounds good," she says quietly as she wipes at her nose.

I press a kiss to the top of her head.

"Sit," I say, motioning at the table. I grab two paper plates from the other side of the kitchen. I join her and hand her a plate as she opens the pizza box. We each grab a slice from the box and begin to eat quietly, Thea picking off the vegetables.

They say actions speak louder than words, and I just hope that for today, this is enough.

# Chapter Nine

## Beth

It's the Fourth of July and I wake up feeling like absolute garbage. I've got a stuffy nose that I can barely breathe out of, a sore throat that feels like razor blades, a heavy chest, and watery eyes — the perfect mixture for a summer cold. I feel poorly enough that I decide to take a sick day and not go into the diner; a rare occurrence for me.

Thea has settled in nicely and I know that between her, Graham, and Raquel, the diner is in good hands today. Besides, we're closing early so that everyone can attend the annual Fourth of July festival later in the day. Driftbay knows how to throw a party when it comes to the Fourth. All of the local establishments shut down around noon to allow everyone the opportunity to experience the party.

All varieties of food trucks come in, there are local vendors set up, carnival games, a giant Ferris wheel, and a marvelous fireworks show at the end of the night. Most folks tend to migrate to the beach to watch the final spectacle, but I tend to stick to watching from my porch. Thea plans to check out the excitement with her friends later.

I fall back asleep shortly after I hear her leave for the morning and wake up a couple of hours later. I'm disoriented for a moment, but I can't ignore the grumbling of my stomach. I get up and stumble to the kitchen, only having enough energy to pop a couple pieces of bread in the toaster and grab the butter from the fridge. While it toasts, I pad down the hallway to the bathroom and flip the light on, searching the medicine cabinet for some ibuprofen for my body aches. Finding it, I shut the mirrored door and dump two pills out into my hand. I run a small glass full of water, put the pills in my mouth and throw my head back, chasing them with the water.

Setting the glass down, I lean against the counter and stare at my reflection. Gone are the youthful days of memories past, though most days I still feel twenty-eight. More and more gray hairs are sprouting, a stark difference compared to their dark brown companions. My face has fine lines and the beginnings of wrinkles, no matter how much expensive cream and serum I use. I can't fight the ticking clock. The bags under my eyes are prominent and harsh. Today is a day I truly *feel* my age.

The toaster dings in the kitchen and I flip the light off in the bathroom before making my way across the house. I grab the toast with one hand and a knife with the other, scooping up pats of butter.

Longing to be back in bed, I toss the pieces of bread onto a paper plate and sit down at the table. I'm able to get a few bites down before I give up and toss my breakfast into the trash can.

I head back to my bedroom and press a hand to my forehead; I think I have a fever. Crawling into bed, I pull the comforter up around my neck and burrow deep in my bed to try to get rid of my chills.

The sound of incessant knocking on my front door raises me from my slumber a while later. I glance at my alarm clock; I've been asleep for three hours.

*If I ignore them long enough, they'll go away,* I think to myself as I reach for another pillow. I fold it over the back of my head, trying to cover my ears with it to drown out the knocking.

Only they don't go away and the knocking doesn't stop. I'm aggravated now, just wanting to rest. I get up and stomp out of my bedroom down the hallway to the door. I instantly soften when I see that it's Charlie, holding a pail of soup from Regiano's and some DVDs.

"I was asleep," I say in apology as I open the door.

"Hey," he says, breathing a sigh of relief as he sees me. "I was about to bust the door down."

"You know where the spare key is," I laugh and it turns into a cough that sets my throat ablaze.

"I noticed you weren't at the diner this morning and Thea said you weren't feeling well, so I brought supplies." He holds up the soup pail and the DVDs. "Chicken gnocchi soup from Regiano's, your favorite, and some cheesy rom-coms guaranteed to make you laugh."

He's dressed in civilian clothes, jeans and a plain T-shirt, but his radio is strapped to his hip. He must be off duty until the festival later.

"Don't you have better things to do than to worry about me?"

He cocks his head to the side. "You should know by now that I'm *always* going to worry about you."

"What did I do to deserve you?" I ask as I step away from the door so he can enter.

Charlie laughs. "Come on, Beth Ann, let's get you feeling better."

He steps across the threshold of my house and waltzes about like he owns the place. I follow him into the kitchen and sit down at the table.

"Nope," he says as he sets the soup on the counter. "Couch." He points in the direction of the living room.

I do as I'm told and get up, trudging out of the kitchen before collapsing onto one end of the couch. I frown down at myself. I'm in my favorite pajamas — an old sweatshirt of Charlie's that I stole years ago and comfy sweatpants that have seen better days.

But it's Charlie. He's seen the worst of me. I'm sure he won't care if my sweatpants have a few holes in them.

He walks back into the living room with a bowl of steaming soup and hands it to me before he crosses to the television above the fireplace. I stare absentmindedly at the urn standing proud in the center of the mantle, next to it, a birthday card Thea placed there. I can't help but wonder what Caroline would make of Charlie and I if she could see this very moment.

I watch as Charlie fiddles with the DVD player for a bit. The soup steams my face as I breathe in the creamy, chicken aroma, beyond glad he brought this to me. I bring the first spoonful to my lips and blow on it to cool it.

"Mmm," I hum, tasting the soup. This is exactly what I needed. I tuck my legs underneath me as I take another bite.

"Good?" he asks over his shoulder. He stands up and reaches for the remote on the coffee table.

"Very." I take another bite, letting it soothe my sore throat.

Charlie walks around the coffee table and back to the couch. He puts his hand on my forehead as he asks, "Do you have a fever?"

"I think so," I mutter. I haven't had the energy to check but suspect so since I had the chills earlier. I tossed and turned all night, waking up in puddles of sweat every couple of hours.

"Have you taken anything?"

"A couple of ibuprofen."

He nods. "Good," he says as he sits down in the middle of the couch beside me. We sit in silence as he presses play on the remote, the trailers playing on the screen in front of us. I devour the bowl of soup and debate asking for more.

"Thank you for this," I say as I set the empty bowl on the coffee table.

"Of course. I was worried about you. It's not like you to not be at the diner."

I nod in agreement. The diner is my life, it seems.

"Are you working tonight?" I ask, gesturing at his attire.

He shakes his head. "Only if they need me. We're hoping for a quiet Fourth this year."

"You shouldn't have said that," I laugh. "It's like saying Macbeth in the theatre."

Charlie smiles. "Maybe. Maybe not."

"If they need you, go. I'm okay," I say. "I'm a big girl and can take care of myself."

*Though it's nice to have someone else take care of you,* the voice in my head says.

Charlie gets up and crosses the living room to the basket of blankets in the corner. He selects one and walks back to the couch and drapes it over me.

"I know," he says, smiling. "But I wanted to be here." He sits back down on the couch.

I cough again, another thought popping into my head. "You never told me how your date went."

The smile fades from his face. "Turns out," he begins, "it wasn't a love connection."

"Oh. I'm sorry."

He shakes his head and looks at me again. "Don't be. I guess...I'm just waiting for the right one."

He presses another button on the remote and nudges me to look at the television as the movie starts.

I dream about Caroline.

The sun glitters off the water as I watch her dance along the shore. The only sound I hear is the lazy lapping of waves. Caroline doesn't seem to notice me, even though I'm standing so close I could reach out and touch her. Her white cotton dress twirls around her ankles as she moves. She doesn't say a word. She just looks happy. Totally, blissfully happy, as if she is somehow renewed. It's a feeling I envy.

She stops dancing and turns to face me; the biggest smile I've ever seen on her face. She takes my hands in hers, her touch featherlight.

"Tell him," she says, her voice as faint as a whisper. "Let him know how you feel."

I open my mouth to object but she stops me, still smiling. She releases my hands and begins dancing again, moving further away from me now. I reach out to grab her hand again but she dances out of reach. I take a step toward her and then another, but every time she seems to slip through my fingers. My feet sink into the sand as I watch her dance along the water's edge until she disappears out of sight.

I wake with a gasp.

"Are you okay?"

I turn at the sound of the voice and see Charlie in the same position, still on his end of the couch. He's looking at me with concerned eyes as I regain my bearings.

"I had a weird dream," I say. "About my sister."

He nods. "You were mumbling her name."

I adjust my position and notice a drool patch on the armrest.

"Oh, my God," I mutter as I wipe at it, Caroline now forgotten.

Charlie laughs as he watches me, the mood lighter now. "You looked too comfortable to move," he adds.

I did sleep a bit more soundly with him on the couch than I did last night.

"You're awake just in time for fireworks," he adds, holding his hand out to me.

He leads me out of the living room and to my front door.

It was late morning when he came by. I'm surprised he is still here, since I've been asleep almost the whole day.

"Is Thea home? Did she stop by?" I ask, trying to get a grip on exactly how much time has passed.

He nods. "She stopped by a few hours ago, but we didn't want to wake you."

We step out onto the porch to watch the fireworks. There's a cool breeze now that the sun has gone down and it feels great on my skin. My fever must have broken hours ago. I need a shower. I want to scrub the sweat sheen off of my skin.

The two of us stay silent as we listen to the folks out on the beach settling in.

"You know, you snore a little when you sleep," Charlie laughs as he looks at me. He's leaning against the railing.

My mouth drops open a little. "I do not," I argue, playfully shoving his shoulder.

He nods. "I find it charming, actually, that such a small person can produce such a large noise."

I cover my face in embarrassment just as the fireworks start. Shimmering, effervescent explosions of color light up the night sky. I have to admit, Driftbay knows how to put on a spectacular fireworks show. I watch them for a while and begin to wonder where Thea is watching them from. I make a mental note to text her when I go back inside and find my phone.

The faint smell of smoke lingers in the air and it tickles my nose. Charlie marvels at the fireworks and it's like watching a little kid on Christmas morning. It's endearing that he takes such delight in them. I catch myself watching him more than the actual fireworks.

We're sitting in a comfortable silence watching the grand finale when I hear his radio go off — a jumbled rattling of a code I can't understand. It instantly gets his attention.

Charlie looks at me with apologetic eyes as he radios back that he will be there as soon as he can.

"I'm sorry," he says. It's almost a whisper. He turns to the house.

"Don't be." I wrap my arms around myself as I shiver. "Duty calls. Besides, you spent all day over here taking care of me."

We walk back into the house and I start toward the living room to grab my dirty dishes from earlier, but they're already gone. I stick my head into the kitchen as Charlie pulls his sneakers on.

"I did your dishes earlier," he says. "Figured you wouldn't feel up to it."

"Thanks," I say as I stare at him. It's been nice experiencing the domestic life with him today. I don't know if it's the sickness, or the dream about Caroline, but my mind is whirling and there's only one thing I want — *need* — to say to him.

I know that if I don't say it now, I never will. The words are coming fast and hard, ready to barrel out of me the second I open my mouth.

"I lied to you," I say. It comes out quietly, my voice subdued by nerves and whatever virus is attacking my immune system.

"Hmm?" he hums. He's fighting with his left sneaker in the doorway.

"I lied," I repeat, growing more confident, "about your date."

Charlie freezes and then slowly looks up at me. I know that whatever happens next has the ability to change the entire trajectory of our friendship forever.

"You...lied," he repeats, the words heavy between us.

"I thought I could deal with it," I say. "But I can't."

He rubs his face with both hands and sighs. I know time isn't on our side, it never has been, but especially now with his work call fighting for his attention.

"So, when I asked you if you were okay with me seeing someone, you lied to my face?"

I pause, my heartbeat thundering in my ears. "Yes," I whisper. I cross my arms in front of my chest as I look at him. "I want you to be happy, but I also don't want to lose you."

"You're not going to lose me." He steps closer to me, the seconds ticking away like a bomb about to explode.

"I didn't want to lose our friendship," I say.

He ponders this for a moment and I see a flash of anger in his eyes. "So, lying to me was the better alternative?"

"At the time, yes." It's a whisper again. "It meant keeping you in my life."

"I can still be in your life and date someone else, Beth. The same goes for you. We've talked about this."

Not hearing 'Ann' cross his lips feels like a slap to the face.

"I want you to be happy," I repeat, fidgeting with the strings of my hoodie now. "I just...want you to be happy...with me."

He stares at me, not hearing what I'm really saying.

"I love you, Charlie."

There. I've said it. There's no going back now. The words are out in the open, unable to be taken back or packed away neatly into some dessert, where I have been hiding them for so long.

His radio goes off again and I jump at the noise. He angrily jams it back into its holster after he repeats that he is on his way. He looks at me once more and motions between us.

"I have to go," he says, and I detect a hint of anger laced in his voice, "but we are *not* done here."

I nod and watch him walk through the door, wondering if he just walked out of my life.

# Chapter Ten

## Thea

Aunt Beth is home sick and the diner is unusually quiet this morning. Everyone in town is getting ready for the big Fourth of July festival later. Graham has been talking about it nonstop for the last week. He's very excited to show me his favorite part of summer in Driftbay.

As usual, Judith comes in for a treat and her morning visit. I take Beth's place, filling a glass of ice water and bringing her a piece of cake. Today's special is angel food cake, decorated to look like the American flag with whipped cream, blueberries, and strawberries. Judith is delighted as I set it down in front of her and take a seat across from her in the booth.

"Morning, dearie," she says.

"Good morning, Judith," I say as I fidget in the seat to get comfortable.

"Are you going to the festival later?" she asks.

I nod. "Graham seems pretty excited to show me around. Are you going?"

"I used to," she says wistfully. "I'm too old now."

"You're never too old for some fun," I say. "You could go with me and Graham."

"Oh, I have my fun," she says, shaking her head, "don't you worry about that. Besides, I don't want to intrude." She takes a bite of her cake and looks at me. "This is delicious, dearie."

I beam. "Thank you." I feel a rush of blood flush my cheeks. I never take compliments well.

"I used to take my son, when he was little," she says. "But he's grown now and moved away. I don't see him often." She frowns as she picks up another bite of cake.

"He didn't want to stay in Driftbay?"

"Oh, heavens no. He hated it here. He wanted to move to a city. Somewhere with more life, he always said."

It's my turn to frown now. "They're not all they're cracked up to be," I mutter, thinking of Seattle.

"He's a senior VP at some company. I'm still not exactly sure what he does." Judith waves her hand in the air. "I just know he stays busy. Sometimes too busy even for his mother."

"I'm sorry."

"Don't be." She smiles. "That's partly why I'm so sweet on that aunt of yours. She always makes time for me."

"She's very fond of you."

"Any word on her and Charlie?" she asks, cutting straight to the point.

"Not that I've heard," I laugh.

She shakes her head and mutters under her breath, "That woman."

"Give her time," I say. "I"m sure she will eventually." I'm not sure why she is so adamant about Beth and Charlie getting together.

We nearly have to shoo Judith from the restaurant in order to close on time. Raquel, Graham, and I finish our duties and lock up before we're free for the afternoon's festivities.

I send Beth a quick text to check in on her and let her know that everything went well at the diner.

After a quick change of clothes, Graham and I walk toward the center of town. Raquel disappeared right after we closed, but said she would meet up with us later.

He wasn't kidding when he said the entire town shuts down for this. We arrive in the town square slightly sweaty from our walk in the blistering sun. Everywhere I look has been transformed into something out of a Hallmark movie. There's a section blocked off for vendors; it's full of local artists and their beautiful creations. It's heartwarming to see Driftbay come together to celebrate its citizens.

Graham leads the way as we walk through the crowd that's slowly forming. He's heading in the direction of the food trucks and I follow after him. I play with my necklace as we walk. It's comforting to be able to wear it again now that I have a new chain for it; a gift from Ireland. I keep waiting for him to hold my hand, but he doesn't. He seems too nervous.

He slows to a stop as we approach a line for a neon green food truck, The Picklenator, and I look up at the sign. It advertises dill pickle pizza, among other pickle pleasantries, and Graham laughs as he sees my face.

"Do you trust me?" he asks, nodding his head in the direction of the sign.

I pause for a moment before I say, "Yes."

We wait in line for about fifteen minutes before we reach the front. The sun has reached its peak, and the heat beats down on us ruthlessly. I know I'll have a sunburn tomorrow. I take a deep breath in, catching whiffs of an assortment of fragrances. The twang of the dill pickles, the pizza crusts baking, as well as the faint sweetness of kettle corn and cotton candy fill my nostrils.

Graham steps up to the window to order and I listen as he orders for us — two slices of dill pickle pizza and two lemon shake ups. We wait for our food for only a few minutes before it's served.

He leads me over to the row of picnic tables across the town square and sits down at one. I join him, sitting down across from him.

"I have waited all year for this," he says as he picks up the piece of pizza. "It was my favorite last year."

I resist taking my first bite so that I can watch him take his. His teeth close around the gooey, cheesy, greasy slice and he closes his eyes.

"Just as good as I remember," he says after he finishes another bite. He grabs a napkin from the dispenser on the table and wipes at his mouth. I'm not a huge fan of pickles, but his excitement is infectious.

I pick up my piece and take a bite. To my surprise, the combination of flavors work well together and it's actually quite good.

"I like it," I say, as Graham beams and hands me a napkin.

"See? Told you to trust me," he says, shoving another bite into his mouth.

We eat in silence for the next couple of moments, the sound of whirling rides and children laughing ringing in our ears.

"I asked Judith if she wanted to join us this afternoon,"I say, tearing off a piece of my crust and popping it into my mouth.

"Oh?" Graham asks.

I nod as I shuffle on the bench. "She mentioned how she used to bring her son when he was younger and I thought it would be nice."

He nods. "Is she coming?"

I shake my head. "No, said she didn't want to intrude."

"She probably thought this was a date." He takes another bite of his pizza.

"Well," I say, "it kind of is, isn't it?" I ask, feeling brave. I reach for my lemon shake up and take a sip.

"Do you want it to be a date?"

"Do you?"

"I asked you first," he retorts.

"Maybe." I smile.

"Well, then." Graham leans across the table. "How about this? When I ask you on a date, you'll know."

"So, it's a matter of 'when' and not 'if'?" I ask.

"Exactly." He smiles as he tears into his pizza again.

I ponder his words as I eat another bite, letting the salty cheese melt in my mouth.

We finish eating and gather our trash, hastily getting out of the way of the growing crowd. Graham reaches for me, holding his hand out.

"Come on," he says. "There's something I want to show you."

I slip my hand into his and my breath catches in my throat at the contact. Our fingers lace together perfectly, as if we had done this a million times.

He leads me away from the food trucks and toward the vendor fair. We walk along at a slow pace, taking in the sights of homemade jewelry, painted canvases, handmade pottery, and so much more. The sweltering sun fades away as I walk with him.

We stop at a vendor booth where a woman with Graham's easy smile is selling homemade canned salsa.

"Mom," he says, motioning at me, "this is my good friend, Thea. Thea, this is my mother, Michele."

I smile as I extend a hand to her. "It's lovely to meet you, Mrs. Gordon."

"Oh, please, call me Michele. Mrs. Gordon reminds me of my ex-husband."

I freeze for a moment, thinking of the day in the kitchen when Graham recounted the tale of his parents' divorce.

Michele laughs, a smile spreading across her face. Her kind, dark brown eyes sparkle as she chuckles. "It's fine," she says as she runs a hand through her spiky dark brown hair. It reminds me of Beth's, but shorter and with less gray around the face.

"Graham has told me so much about you," she says, putting her hand on her hip. "I think he might even be a little sweet on you."

"Mom," Graham says under his breath, a touch embarrassed. His cheeks start to turn pink. He grabs my arm and pulls me closer to him. "We're leaving now."

Michele chuckles as Graham pulls me away from her salsa stand and we continue walking.

"Sorry about that," he says after he lets go of me. He wrings his hands together nervously.

"So," I say. "Not a date, but I just met your mom?" A smile tugs at the corners of my mouth.

"Again," he says, "when it's a date, you'll know." We walk out of the vendor fair and Graham steers us toward the carnival. The sun blazes down on us as we come to a stop at the cornhole station.

"Want to play?" he asks as he stops. "I'm a master at cornhole, if I do say so myself."

I laugh. "Sure."

Graham steps up to the boards and starts grabbing the bean bags from the ground. He hands me the yellow set while he takes the green, and walks over to his board. I take a step up to mine and get into place. I let him throw first, since he is the master, after all.

He tosses his first bean bag and it makes a loud thud as it lands on the board and slides through the hole. He cheers, pumping his fist in the air, and I laugh before tossing mine out. It falls short of the board, skidding across the grass.

"Told you," I say, "no athletic ability."

Graham focuses on tossing his next bean bag, another winner that sinks through the hole in the board. He comes over to me and stands behind me, and reaches for my throwing arm.

"Here," he says, lightly gripping my arm. We move in tandem as he gently pulls my arm back. The contact makes my skin tingle.

"Just...like...this." He guides me through the motion of throwing the bean bag and we watch as it slides through the hole in my board.

"See?" Graham asks. "Not too bad."

"Thanks," I say. I meet his eyes and for a moment, I think that *now* he's going to kiss me.

My concentration is broken when something behind him shifts and comes into focus. I freeze, the smile fading from my face.

"What?" he asks, turning to follow my gaze.

"Is that Jake?" I whisper.

I squint my eyes as I stare across the festival at Jake and a blonde-haired girl. I feel like I've seen her before and it takes me a moment to place her. It hits me that I have seen her before. It's Emily, the waitress from the tavern.

Graham drops the bean bags and his hands ball into fists at his side.

"I'm going to say something," he says.

"No, don't," I plead, turning back to him. "His dad threatened Beth and I really don't want to cause a scene."

"His dad threatened Beth?" he echoes.

I nod. "Yeah, it was a whole ordeal."

"He shouldn't get away with what he did to you."

"No, but it's better if we don't engage." I bend down and pick up the bean bags. "Come on, let's finish our game. Just ignore him."

I hand him his bean bags and nudge him back toward the game.

Graham half heartedly throws a bean bag and still makes the shot.

"Not fair," I say, trying to make him laugh.

"I think you're being bad on purpose."

"Oh, I promise you I'm not."

I glance over my shoulder again and see Emily by herself now at the ticket stand. This might be my only chance to speak to her.

"I'll be right back," I tell Graham before dropping my bean bags and darting off through the crowd.

She's just turning away from the ticket stand when I catch up to her.

"Hi," I say as I tuck my hair behind my ear. "Emily, right?"

She looks up at me, confused.

"Yeah," she answers warily.

“You’re here with Jake Osborne?”

“Who are you?” she asks.

I shake my head. “Not important. Look,” I say, stepping closer to her. “I don’t want to tell you what to do, but please be careful with him.”

“Wait, I remember you,” she says, “from the tavern.”

I nod and glance around again. I know I don’t have much time before Jake reappears.

“Yes, that’s me. I just wanted to warn you that Jake isn’t the nice guy he comes off as at first. He groped me that night at the tavern.”

Emily’s face twists into a look of disgust. “Oh my God,” she says.

“He kept trying to kiss me and wasn’t taking no for an answer,” I explain. “So, again, whatever you do, just be careful with him.”

Emily glances over her shoulder and I follow her gaze, spotting Jake leaning up against a gate around one of the carnival rides.

“Noted,” she says, looking back at me. “Thanks for the heads up.”

“You’re welcome.” I smile.

She nods and I dart back across the festival to Graham, who is still playing cornhole by himself.

“What was that about?” he asks.

“Just doing what Raquel tried to do for me,” I say. I snatch a bag from his hand. “Now, prepare to get stomped.”

It's nearly sunset when we decide to ride the Ferris wheel. It's slow going to the top, but I get a chance to take in a new view of Driftbay. The whole town sprawls out in front of me and it's breathtaking. I can see the diner from up here and the cottage on the edge of the beach.

"Wow," I breathe, as I take it all in.

Graham shuffles in the seat and puts his arm around me. "It's pretty magnificent, isn't it?"

I nod. I bite the inside of my cheek as images of my mom flood my brain. I wish she were here to see this.

"Hey," he says quietly. "You okay?"

"Yeah," I say, my voice shaking. "Just thinking about my mom."

He pulls me closer to his side. "There might not be much here, but what's here is enough," he says.

I think about his words and how true they are. Driftbay is definitely the smallest town I've ever lived in, but I wouldn't trade it for anything. I've met some of the kindest people within these city limits.

We begin our descent just as the sun begins hers. I'm grateful to be here with Graham. He's never pushy and always meets me where I am.

We climb out of the carriage to find Raquel waiting for us at the gate, tapping her foot. She breaks into a smile when she sees us.

"Hey!" she exclaims. "Sorry about earlier, I got tied up."

Graham just nods at her explanation.

"A friend of mine is having a party a couple of blocks away. You want to go?" she asks.

"I'm actually going to go help my mom pack up her booth," he says as he points behind him.

I was hoping the two of us would head to the beach to watch the fireworks. I look back at Raquel and shrug.

"Sure. I'll go," I say.

The two of us say goodbye to Graham and then take off on foot in the direction of the party, away from the town square and excitement. We walk a couple of blocks as Raquel tells me about her afternoon. We're heading toward a part of Driftbay that I haven't explored before.

I can hear the bass from the music long before we even reach the two-story house. I'm surprised it's allowed to be that loud in town. We walk through the front door and Raquel excitedly greets a couple of her friends. There's smoke everywhere and I'm not sure if it's from cigarettes, or weed, or both.

Raquel disappears into the house with a few of her friends. I look around; I don't know anyone here besides her. I duck into the kitchen and find a bowl of cherry punch on the counter, next to some matching red cups. Dodging people, I walk over and help myself to a glass. It's sweet, and doesn't taste like it has alcohol in it, but of course, I know better than that.

I quickly drink my first glass, feeling awkward at this party, like I don't belong. I wish Graham had come with us. Anxiety is clawing at the back of my throat, ready to suffocate me at any given moment.

I dip out another glass and take a drink, feeling the familiar warmth spreading throughout my body.

The music changes and for a moment, all I hear are the conversations happening around me. Even that is still too much. I gulp down my second glass, waiting for my body to loosen up, for the anxiety to subside. I refill my glass a third time before I head outside for some fresh air.

There's a sliding glass door on the opposite side of the kitchen. It's unlocked and slides open easily, granting me access to the backyard. I jog down the back porch steps and sit down on one of them, willing myself to calm down. I take deep breaths and finish my third glass of punch. I debate leaving but I also don't want to leave Raquel here.

The music, crowd, and atmosphere proved to be a bit too much for me, but the fresh air is helping. The music is muffled now that I'm outside and there's just a couple of partygoers in the backyard.

The sky erupts into bursts of shimmering color and I stare up at it. I had hoped Graham and I could watch the fireworks from the beach, but maybe next time. I wonder if Beth is watching them, too.

I take another sip of my drink and realize it's empty. I set the cup next to me on the step. The movement makes me dizzy and I realize how tipsy I am. I'm not sure I could walk a straight line given the chance. I'm rooted to my seat on the steps as I watch the fireworks, in a buzzed, blissful state.

The music in the house stops abruptly, but it;s hard to focus on anything except the sparkling sky. The sliding glass door opens and a booming voice startles me, making me jump out of my skin.

"Put your hands up!"

I know that voice. I lurch to my feet, staggering as I raise my hands in the air and turn around. A flashlight is roving the backyard and I squint as it moves over my face. It trails down to my feet and lands on the red cup.

I can see red and blue lights flashing from the front of the house and spot an officer in the kitchen through the window.

I don't know where Raquel is. I don't know what to do. Running will get me in trouble but staying rooted in place will surely get me in even more.

"Thea," I hear. It's the same voice, only softer and my stomach drops.

It's not just any cop.

It's Charlie.

He walks toward me and grips my forearms, steadying me as I sway.

"Hey, Charlie," I mutter, meeting his intense blue eyes for a moment before looking down at my feet. They're like Beth's in that sense, an icy blue, sharp enough to cut, and it's like he can see straight through me.

My alcohol-induced buzz withers under his scrutiny.

"What the hell do you think you're doing?" he hisses.

I shrug.

"Walk a straight line," he says as he releases my arms. He nods toward the grass.

I do as he says, or at least, I attempt to. I giggle as I teeter on the grass.

"Thea," he repeats. "Come on." He reaches for me and twists my arms behind my back.

"Am I going to jail?" I ask.

"No, you're going to your aunt."

A chill runs down my spine. I don't know which option is worse.

"Listen to me," he says, his voice low. "I'm going to take you to my squad car and then I'm taking you to Beth Ann."

Charlie leads me around the front of the house, passing another officer and party-goer.

"I'll be back," he says as he leads me to his squad car. He opens the back door for me to get in. Wordlessly, I fumble with the buckle as Charlie shuts the door on me and walks around to the driver's side.

"Beth Ann isn't going to like this," he says as he catches my eyes in the rear view mirror.

"I know," I mumble. It was cute at first to hear him call her Beth Ann, but now it's just annoying. I settle my gaze on the yard in front of me, watching officers lead out more underage drinkers. I blink my eyes in time with the flash of the lights on their cars to focus.

The ride home is quiet. There's no music playing through the car and Charlie has his radio turned down low. I can hear a few more calls go out but I can't make out what they say.

Charlie doesn't speak to me as he drives, and I know he's disappointed in me.

We arrive at Beth's cottage and he kills the engine.

"Well," he says, "might as well get this over with."

Whether it's delivering me or seeing Beth's reaction, I'm not sure.

He gets out of the car and comes around to open my door. He slams it shut behind me and we trudge up the porch steps. I fumble with my keys but Charlie bangs on the door with his fist before I can find the right one.

Aunt Beth opens the door a minute later. She looks between us and then her expression ices over.

"Tell me," she says, keeping her voice even, "that this is not what I think it is."

"I'm sorry, Beth Ann," Charlie says. "I brought her here before anyone else found her."

Her eyes slide over to me and if looks could kill, I'd be dead on the spot. There's a ferocity in her eyes that I haven't seen before. I break the gaze, looking down at my feet.

"Thea," she says, commanding me to look at her again.

I meet her gaze but offer no explanation. My head is still spinning.

"I'll take it from here," she says to Charlie, coughing as she reaches for me. She pulls me through the doorway and I wait for her to yell. She says something else to Charlie under her breath. I flinch at the sound of the slamming door a second later.

"Thea," she repeats, sniffling through her cold. She crosses her arms over her chest. "What the hell has gotten into you?"

Again, I offer no explanation.

"Are you going to speak or are you suddenly mute?" she snaps.

"What do you want me to say?" I ask.

"Why?" she asks, a hint of desperation in her voice. "I thought we were past this."

"It's nothing," I say. I set my phone on the table in the entryway as it buzzes. "It was just a party."

"No. Don't you dare tell me it's nothing. This is you drowning right in front of me and I'm not going to let that happen."

"I was just...really anxious tonight," I say, "and it helps loosen me up."

She frowns. "What does that mean?"

"It helps soothe the anxiety. I can be someone fun and carefree, not someone who's just sad all the time."

"Oh, Thea." I can tell she wants to hug me but refrains. "You can be that person without alcohol, you just have to learn how." She steps closer to me. "You think it's making it better? It's not. And I can't..." she shakes her head, "I won't lose you, too. I don't care how angry you get at me for saying this, but I think you need real help. I think you should see a therapist."

"Oh, come on," I start, but she cuts me off. My phone buzzes again against the table and we both glance at it.

Beth looks back at me. "No. I don't want to hear it. You may legally be an adult but..." she pauses. "I'm letting you live here for free. As long as you live under my roof, you will abide by my rules."

"You're not my mom," I spit out, crossing my arms over my chest.

"Don't you think I know that? Trust me, I'm well aware that I'm not." She sneezes.

"Oh, I'm sorry. Did I burden you by coming here?"

"Thea, you know that's not true."

"You're not the martyr for taking in your dead sister's daughter." The words are venom spewing from my lips but I can't stop them. I see Beth recoil from them before she steps closer, closing the distance between us.

"Need I remind you that you are *not* the only person who lost someone that day," she says. "I also lost my sister. So, even though you're drowning in grief, take a look around and see that you're not alone in it. I'm right there in that ocean with you."

I stay silent, anger radiating off of me in waves as she continues. I hear my phone buzz once more against the table.

"I think it's best that you start seeing a therapist. Someone to help you. I'll see one, too, if that would help. You cannot use alcohol to drown out your grief and anxiety. You can have fun without it. It doesn't have to be a crutch."

Her words pack a punch.

"Better than ending up like you," I mutter.

"What is that supposed to mean?" There's fire in her eyes.

"At least I have fun. You're a slave to your job and have been in love with a man for thirty-five years who's none the wiser. Sounds miserable to me."

As soon as I've said the words, I know they're too much, that I've gone too far. I see Beth tense, anger consuming her whole.

"You *will* see a therapist and get help. End of discussion." She uncrosses her arms and rubs her temples as my phone vibrates again. "Who on God's green earth is texting you so much?" she yells.

I swipe my phone from the table and glance at the homescreen full of messages from Graham.

"Graham," I mutter.

"Look, Thea, I love you, but you are making it very hard."

"Sorry," I say, in a tone that's anything but. I turn on my heels and head for my room, tears welling in my eyes. I shut the door behind me and lean against it, trying a breathing technique I saw on the internet to calm myself down. I repeat the process a few times, wondering how we ended up here.

And for the first time, I wonder if coming to Driftbay was one giant mistake.

I'm up early the next morning after tossing and turning all night, knowing I need to apologize to Aunt Beth. Unfortunately for me, she's already gone by the time I get up.

I walk to the diner in silence, following my usual route. Driftbay is calm at this time of day, especially after the festival last night. It's already stifling out so I throw my hair up into a ponytail as I walk.

Graham is in the kitchen when I arrive, rolling silverware for the day.

"Hey," he says as he sees me, a smile appearing on his face.

"Hi," I say, before ducking into the back room to ditch my keys and phone. Walking back into the kitchen, I grab my apron and tie it around my waist.

"How was the party last night?"

I groan and it makes me realize my head has been pounding since I got up.

"I don't really want to talk about it," I say.

"Oh." Graham's smile fades.

"Let's just say that I should have helped you and your mom," I offer.

"She enjoyed meeting you," he says, grabbing another napkin and a bunch of utensils.

"She's a sweet lady." I glance around and change the subject. "Is Beth around?"

Graham jerks his head in the direction of her office. "Doing the deposit," he says, "but be careful, she's in a mood."

I nod, knowing I'm the reason for her anger. I head to the pantry and pull out my ingredients and get to work making the basics — chocolate chip cookies and brownies, recipes I know like the back of my hand. My mind whirls. I definitely overdid it last night and need to apologize.

I wait until the last moment possible to take the treats up to the display case in the front of the diner. I'm hoping to catch Beth by herself as she loads in the cash register for the day.

Unfortunately, I catch sight of fiery red hair instead of smooth dark chocolate brown at the register. Penny is loading it in.

"No Beth?" I ask as I look around.

"She's in the office," Penny says as she shakes her head. "Something about schedule changes and then a delivery truck broke down and won't be here today."

I nod slowly.

This day is going to be longer than I thought.

It feels like Beth avoids me all morning, but I know she's dealing with more than our family issues today. Our normal delivery truck has now been pushed back by two days and she's running around checking inventory. I stay out of her way, not wanting to break her concentration as she scribbles away on her notepad.

I'm off at noon, like usual, and quietly gather my belongings from the back room. Graham is working a double today. We exchange goodbyes and he waves at me with his spatula like he did the very first day we met.

I punch out, bid farewell to Penny, and then quietly slip out the back of the diner. The sun is scorching and it's quite muggy out as I begin my walk home. I see children playing on a Slip-N-Slide in the front yard of one of the homes I pass by and it reminds me of my first walk to the diner.

I get to the cottage, grab the mail, and walk up the porch steps to the door. Unlocking it, I walk inside. I toss the mail and my wallet on the table in the entryway.

Beth won't be home until later this evening, so I know I have a few free hours to clean the house, a gesture to say I'm sorry. I do some laundry, dust the living room, take out the trash, and bake her favorite dessert — Oreo truffles.

I mix up some icing in her favorite color, purple, and arrange the truffles on a platter where I can write across them. I shove the icing into a pastry bag and begin writing 'I'm sorry' across them. I'm just finishing when she comes home. I hear the metal clink of her keys in the bowl on the entryway table and as she shuffles, taking off her shoes.

My heart is about to beat out of my chest as I wait for her to round the corner into the kitchen. She finally does, but doesn't make eye contact with me. She's rubbing at her wrists and pops her neck before she finally looks up. It's silent for a moment as we both stand there staring at each other across the kitchen. Finally, I find the courage to speak.

"I'm sorry," I begin, "for last night. I was really mean and out of line and I'm really sorry."

Beth continues to stare at me. "We were both angry," she says, choosing her words carefully. "Everything still stands, but I do accept, and appreciate, your apology."

I nod and turn around to grab the tray of truffles. I turn around and present them to her. She reads what I've written on top and a smile slowly spreads across her face. She takes the tray and sets it back on the counter before turning to embrace me. Her cherry-almond scent envelops me as we hug and I get the sense that we will be okay.

It's a week after what I've dubbed "The Incident" when Beth walks into the living room after work and says, "I've made an appointment for you with a therapist."

I close the book I'm reading, a new hobby I've picked up in the last week. "Okay," I say. "Thank you."

"Tomorrow at ten. There was a cancellation and they were able to get you in quickly.

I nod my head. "Okay," I repeat. There's no use in fighting it. I know she's right. I need to see someone. I need help navigating this.

"I took off from the diner so I could go with you," she says as she sits down beside me on the couch.

"Thank you," I say, because I know it's a big deal for her to miss work.

"I told Raquel and Graham that you wouldn't be in, either, but not to worry."

I nod as she turns the television on and shuffles around, getting comfortable. We both stare longingly at the mantle underneath the TV, at the urn front and center on it. It's silver and simple, but perfectly my mom. Beth leans her head onto my shoulder.

"She'd be proud of you for getting help," she says. It's almost a whisper but I still hear it.

"She'd be proud of you for making me," I say and we both laugh.

The next morning, we drive across town to the hospital. The therapist I'm supposed to see has an office on one of the upper level floors. We pull into the parking lot and I stare up at the daunting building, feeling anxiety rise in my chest.

"You okay?" Beth asks as she puts the car in park.

"Not really," I say truthfully. "But it's a start."

"I'm right here with you."

We get out of the car and silently walk together to the hospital's main entrance. We take the elevator up a few floors before we reach another unit for the psychiatric unit.

Beth leads the way as we head to Office 513 — Amber Atherton.

She helps me fill out the required new patient paperwork and waits with me until my name is called.

"I'll be right here," she murmurs as I stand up. Her fingers graze my wrist. "You've got this."

"I've got this," I repeat.

A tall, thin woman stands in the doorway. She smiles as she sees me. "My name is Doctor Atherton," she says, "but you can call me Amber."

"Hi," I say quietly as I stand.

Her soft, kind brown eyes twinkle as she motions for me to follow her. She's got hair the same color as my mom. She's definitely not what I expected for a therapist. I assumed it would be a balding old man in a white coat.

Amber leads me down the hallway to her office and closes the door behind us. I take a seat in front of her desk and feel my heart rate start to speed up. I start to wish Beth had come back with me.

"So," Amber begins as she sits, "What brings you here today?"

*My aunt thinks I'm a drowning alcoholic following the sudden death of my mom,* I think to myself.

I take a shaky breath before I begin.

"Well," I start, fidgeting in the seat. "My mom died in a car accident in January and my aunt thinks I need help dealing with the grief."

Amber nods. "That's a good place to start. So, that's why your aunt wanted you to come. Why did *you* want to come? I assume you wanted to, or else you wouldn't be sitting here. You're an adult, after all."

I hadn't really given it much thought, besides not wanting to disappoint Beth.

"I didn't want to disappoint her," I say quietly.

Amber nods. "Okay," she says, "but could it also be that a part of you wants to be here, too?"

I stare at the carpet.

"You could say that," I say.

"Tell me about yourself," she says gently.

I sigh and shuffle in my seat. "Well, I just moved here a few weeks ago. I used to live in Seattle with my mom."

"I've always wanted to visit Seattle."

"It was nice, but I needed a change. Everything was a constant reminder of what I've lost."

Amber nods again and writes something down on the legal pad in front of her.

"Tell me about your support system."

"Well, before Mom died, it was her, my aunt, my best friend, Ireland," I say. "I had some other friends at school, but they all abandoned me after I left school."

"What were you studying?"

I shuffle in my seat again. "Just generals. I'm not sure what I want to do with my life. My mom was a neurosurgeon, so I've always felt the pressure to make something great of myself."

"It's never easy to live in your parent's shadow."

"No." I shake my head as the room grows silent. " I, uh...bake a lot," I say.

"That's good." She nods to encourage me to keep going. "That's a healthy outlet. Doing something with your hands and creating something out of nothing. What do you like to bake?"

"Everything," I say. "I always toyed with the idea of having my own bakery. Kind of like my aunt Beth. She owns Beth Ann's Diner across town."

"Oh, my husband and I love that place." She smiles brightly. "It's such a cute, quaint little diner. It's my favorite breakfast place."

I smile politely as silence settles between us again.

"Recently I started," I pause, "drinking to help with the grief." I play with my hands in my lap.

Amber's expression changes. "Alcohol is not the answer, but I understand why you were leaning on it. Let me be clear, I am not shaming you." She leans forward in her chair. "When we go through such a profound loss, we do what we can to hold on."

I nod. She gets it.

"It makes the pain go away, when baking doesn't." I shrug. "I'm having nightmares about the car wreck. It's always the same one. No one comes to help and I watch her bleed out in front of me. I scream and scream, but no one can hear me."

Amber writes something down on her notepad again.

"Tell me more about the wreck," she says gently.

"It was winter. We were out shopping, had dinner, and were on our way home. It had been snowing and the roads were slick. It was my idea to go out that day." I pause, the memories flashing through my brain.

"Take your time," Amber encourages me.

"Some guy blew through a stop sign and t-boned us," I slowly continue. "The paramedics say Mom died on impact."

"I'm so sorry."

"Sometimes I feel guilty for surviving. My mom was a neurosurgeon, one of the top in the field. I just..." I trail off as tears form in my eyes. I try to blink them away but they're too fast and they fall down my face.

Amber leans forward and hands me a box of tissues.

The tears fall faster and faster and before I know it, I'm falling apart. My shoulders shake as a sob escapes my mouth and I do my best to reign it in and get myself under control again.

It's a while before I continue. It's embarrassing to cry like this in front of a stranger but Amber's presence is soothing.

"I just like to bake and have no idea what I'm doing with my life. Sometimes I feel like everyone would be better off if I had been the one that died instead of my mom."

"Oh, Thea," she says. She looks at me empathetically. "I know we just met, but I can tell you that is simply not true. Your aunt certainly wouldn't be better off without you."

"Yeah, but she'd have her sister," I say before I blow my nose.

"It sounds like she loves you very much, to insist on bringing you here."

I stay quiet for a moment before I add, "She's been so strong for me, but I know it's consuming her, too."

"Survivor's guilt is completely normal. As is the recurring nightmares. What you went through was very traumatic. And moving across the country, meeting new people...it's a lot of change in a short amount of time."

"You're telling me," I laugh before I blow my nose again. "Beth just thinks I need some help and...she might be right."

"There's no shame in asking for help, Thea," Amber says. "Losing a loved one is never easy." She offers a gentle smile and goes back to her notepad. "You've taken a big step by coming here." She smiles at me and it feels like a warm hug.

"I won't lie and say that this will be a walk in the park," she continues, "but you have to be serious about this, Thea. The sun will shine again."

"The sun will shine again," I repeat before wiping at my tear-stained face.

We talk for a while longer; the hour goes by quicker than I thought it would. Talking with her is comforting; like I'm talking to someone I've known my entire life.

Amber glances at the clock.

"I hate to say this, but our hour is up. Here." She reaches across her desk for a sticky note and jots something down on it before she hands it to me. "I wrote my cell phone number down for you. Day or night, if you need something, I want you to reach out. I'm here for you."

I like her. There's something comforting in her demeanor. Almost like I see a piece of my mom in her. I make a mental note to tell Beth she should see her, too.

"I want to see you back next week," she says. She schedules my next appointment and grabs some pamphlets from the wall behind her. "And I want you to stop drinking. If you feel the urge, lean on your people. Even me, okay?"

I nod.

She stands and I follow suit. I feel emotionally drained and just want to go to bed.

Amber looks at me for a moment and then steps around her desk, opening her arms wide. She gives me a quick hug before motioning to her door.

"It was really great to meet you," she says as we walk out of her office, "and really, if you need anything, please let me know. I'm in your corner."

"Thank you," I say before I walk back out to Beth, who's playing a game on her phone.

"Well?" she asks as she tosses it into her purse.

"It went well," I say, clutching the pamphlets and papers. "I think you'd like her, too."

"Good." Beth breathes a sigh of relief and stands up from her seat. "I'll make an appointment with her, too," she says as she walks toward the receptionist's desk.

I wait off to the side as she speaks with the receptionist. Beth pulls out her phone again and quickly types in her own appointment before she turns to me.

"Ready?" she asks.

I nod.

The elevator ride is quiet and I feel lighter once we reach the parking lot. I bask in the sunshine as we walk to the car and think that for once, it feels like the sun is shining on my life again.

# Chapter Eleven

## Beth

Charlie and I haven't had time to discuss how we left things before he busted that party on the Fourth of July, and I'm anxious to continue the conversation. The last week and a half has been awful with my delivery truck getting off-schedule, recovering from my cold, the aftermath of my fight with Thea, and trying to make her appointments. He's understood that whatever we are is on the back-burner right now.

I just dropped Thea off at another therapy appointment. I venture back out to the car while I wait and text Charlie, asking him to meet me in the parking lot if he isn't busy.

I'm sitting in the car, anxiously scanning the lot for any sign of him. I watch as his squad car pulls in and he looks around, searching for my vehicle. He catches sight of me and slowly drives over to park beside me. He cuts the engine and then tentatively gets out. Shutting the door behind him, he leans against the car. I get out of mine and do the same.

The sky above us is overcast. The weather forecast is calling for a thunderstorm this morning and it seems to be making its way across Driftbay. I can smell it. When you've lived here as long as I have, you can just tell when trouble is rolling in.

"Hey," Charlie says quietly, breaking the silence between us.

"Hi." I fidget with the hem of my shirt, avoiding his eyes. "Thanks for meeting me. Life has just been crazy lately."

From Raquel's report, he hasn't been in the diner for a couple of days, giving me space.

"Of course." He pauses before approaching the next subject. "How's Thea doing?"

I sigh. "She's better than when you last saw her." It's a lame attempt to make him laugh. "Thank you, for bringing her home that night, by the way. She started seeing a therapist last week."

"Good, good." His eyes travel across the parking lot and he clears his throat. We both stand there awkwardly, unsure of how to carry on. We've been dancing around this line for years.

"So, you wanted to talk?" Charlie asks, taking the lead like he always does.

"Yes," I say, crossing my arms over my chest, trying to hug myself in comfort. "No," I sigh, "I don't know." I let out an awkward laugh in an effort to ease the newfound tension between us.

He laughs, but it's strained. "Beth Ann..." he trails off.

"I know." I shake my head in agreement. "We need to." I shuffle my feet. I don't know why this is so hard. This is Charlie, my best friend. I can talk to him about anything.

So why can't I tell him I've loved him for years?

"How about I start?" He reaches for my hand and I uncross my arms. He takes my hand in his and runs his thumb over my knuckles. The contact makes my skin tingle under his touch.

Charlie stands tall and proud against his squad car; if he's anxious, he's not showing it. I, on the other hand, can't quit squirming under his gaze.

"You lied to me," he says, his voice gravelly, "numerous times."

"I did. I own that and I'm sorry." I feel like I'll be saying that a lot during this conversation.

He clears his throat again before he asks, "Why did you lie about being upset that I was going on a date?"

"I think you know why," I say. I've already admitted that I love him; it doesn't take a rocket scientist to figure out why I'd be upset that he went on a date with someone else.

"I want to hear your explanation. I think I'm owed that much."

I swallow before I answer. "You're right. I realized I had feelings for you years ago. Big feelings. I didn't know what to do with them. I was scared that if I acted on them, you wouldn't reciprocate, and it would ruin our friendship. You're my stability." I steady my stance now and push off the car. "I couldn't bear the thought of losing you, so I decided that if having you as my best friend was the best I could get, then so be it. I'd deal with it. And it worked for a while."

He nods slowly to get me to continue. "Until I got together with someone else," he finishes.

"I thought lying about it would keep the peace. Keep you in my life if things got serious between you and some other woman."

"Beth Ann, I'll always be in your life." Charlie smiles. "You can't get rid of me. You should know that by now."

"I know," I say, smiling slightly. I glance down at our connected hands. "I just get anxious sometimes."

Thunder claps in the distance and we both glance up at the darkening sky.

"Losing Caroline and everything going on with Thea, and hell, even Judith has been on me about it. It's just all shown me that life really is short and that I truly do love you. Look, Charlie, you've been my best friend since college. You are one of the most important people in my life. I don't want to do anything that jeopardizes that. I don't think I could survive without you."

"That will never happen," he mutters as he reaches up and tucks a strand of hair behind my ear. "Besides, it was never going to work out with someone else."

"Why's that?" I ask. I look up to meet his gaze, and our eyes lock.

"Because I love you, too, Beth Ann."

Relief washes over me at the sound of those words and for a moment, I don't believe I've heard him correctly.

My heart flutters in my chest and I can't stop the smile that starts spreading across my face. For so long, I've wanted to hear those words hang from his lips, to know that my feelings are reciprocated.

"It was never going to work with anyone else, because it's always been you. Even though you've been stubborn enough to not let me love you all these years. Won't you let me?"

The sky above us starts weeping. Raindrops plummet to the ground, splattering all around. I feel my hair start to dampen and droplets cling to my eyelashes.

"I'm scared, Charlie," I say.

"Scared of what?" he pleads. "Let yourself be happy."

"What if it doesn't work out?" My voice is small. "I'm not sure we could survive going back to just being friends."

"But what if it does?" He grips my hand tighter now. "I have looked for fragments of you in every woman I've dated since I met you. I've loved you for over three decades. Let me."

I open my mouth for a rebuttal but then his lips are on mine and the line that's separated us for thirty-five years dissolves in the rain splattering around us. My heart is in my throat and I feel like I'm going to combust now that these emotions are out in the open. We pull apart, staring at each other with hungry expressions as the rain continues to fall.

"I love you," he repeats. The words hang heavily in the air, unable to be retrieved. "And I'm sorry that it took me this long to say it."

He leans his forehead against mine as I laugh, tears of joy spilling over my eyes.

"I think we owe it to ourselves to give it a shot and see this through, don't you? What we could make of this," he pulls away and motions between us, "of us." Gently, he reaches for my face and his thumbs wipe away my tears.

"I'm sorry for lying to you," I whisper.

"I understand why you did." The radio on his hip goes off, startling me.

"Meet me at Regiano's tonight at eight, if you're committed to giving us a chance. I'll be there. Will you?"

I nod, unable to speak.

He leans forward and gently presses his lips to my forehead. He gives my forearms a comforting squeeze before he opens his car door and gets back in the car. I give him a little wave as I watch him flip the police lights on and drive away.

My fingertips graze my lips, still tingling from Charlie's kiss. I feel like a teenager again, excited about tonight and relieved that it didn't blow up in my face.

I wipe at my eyes and blink a few times before I get back in my car. I lean my head back, gripping the steering wheel with both hands while I wait for Thea. My mind is whirling, replaying what just happened, but I'm doing my best to focus on one thing.

Charlie loves me, in a way I didn't expect him to, and that...means everything.

I stand in my bedroom, staring at the closet. Butterflies dance in my stomach as my eyes scan the articles of clothing before me. I shouldn't be this nervous. I shouldn't be nervous at all. The man I'm meeting tonight has seen me through all my highs and lows, thick and thin, good and bad.

*It does not matter what dress I wear,* I think to myself.

Only it does. Because *he* will be there.

*"Meet me at Regiano's tonight, if you're committed to giving us a chance."*

I pull a short dress from the back of my closet, navy with a bright floral pattern and a bright red, satin ribbon around the waist. I'd been saving it for a special occasion. I rip the tags off, toss them onto my dresser, and slide it on. It fits me like a glove. I glance at my reflection in the mirror and take a moment to admire myself. Dare I say, I look good.

My hair falls in soft curls around my face and there's a rosy, girlish hint of rouge to my cheeks. My eyes sparkle as they stare back at me and I feel the excitement building. I'm buzzing with energy.

Thea stops in the doorway as I'm putting my earrings in. I watch her reflection through the mirror and she smiles.

"You look beautiful," she says as she shoves off the doorframe and enters the room.

"Thank you." I clasp the earring shut and turn around so she can see the full effect.

She gently lays her overnight bag down on my bed — she's having a sleepover with Raquel tonight — before she walks over to me.

"Here," she says softly, spinning me back around. Her fingers reach for my zipper and she carefully zips me up. "Charlie is a lucky man."

I feel myself blush as I turn back to face her. "Thank you," I repeat. My emotions take over and I pull her into a hug.

"What's that for?" she asks when we separate.

I shrug. "I just love ya, kid."

Thea smiles and reaches for her bag. "I'll check in when I get to Raquel's," she says, "but I don't want to bug you on your date."

I nod. "Okay. Be safe. Make good choices!"

"Have fun," she says as she walks to the door. "Get a good story to tell Judith!" she adds before she ducks around the corner. I hear her giggle as she makes her way to the front door.

I can't help but roll my eyes as I turn to my dresser and select my perfume. I spritz it onto my neck and wrists before spraying some in my hair for extra measure.

At ten to eight, I take a deep breath and leave the house, after getting confirmation from Thea that she made it safely to Raquel's. The drive to Regiano's is just a few minutes; Driftbay isn't that big. I meet Charlie right at eight, butterflies fluttering through my stomach the entire drive there.

I park beside his SUV and get out of my vehicle. He's leaning against the hood of his car. His eyes slowly travel down my body and I can't help but blush at the attention. It makes me feel confident, knowing that after all these years, I can still draw a man's gaze.

"Beth Ann," he whispers as he looks at me, "You look beautiful."

"Thank you." I drink in the sight of him — he's wearing dark wash jeans and my favorite gray button down, the one that makes me go weak in the knees. Gray is his color. It makes his skin look tan and his dark blue eyes pop.

"You don't look too bad yourself," I add.

He reaches a hand out toward me and I take it. He gently spins me around so he can get the full view before he pushes off the car and pulls me into his side. I catch a whiff of him; he smells luxurious, like pomegranates and sandalwood.

"Is that a new cologne?" I ask as we walk toward the restaurant entrance.

He shrugs. "I save it for special occasions. Thanksgiving, Christmas, dates with my girl."

"Your girl, huh?"

"Is that cheesy?" he asks as he opens the door for me.

I pretend to ponder it. "Little bit."

We walk in together and I swear that I see a few heads turn. Everyone in town knows us, the diner owner and the sheriff. This is also what I'm afraid of — everyone knowing *about* us. And the rumors that will swirl if we don't get this right and this...whatever this is, fails.

His hand finds the small of my back as our waitress leads us out onto the patio, per his request. It's a beautiful summer evening; the setting sun paints the sky a stunning mosaic of colors. The air is warm but not stifling, and the patio is inviting and cozy. Fairy lights twinkle above us, casting a soft glow across the patio, and there's potted plants all around.

Charlie pulls out my chair at the table, a true gentleman, before he sits in his own.

"You have to admit, this is a little weird," I say, trying to break the ice. "I mean, us...here..." I gesture between us.

He laughs. "It's different, yes, but it's a good kind of different." His eyes linger on me for a moment and I feel my cheeks start to burn.

"Don't look at me like that," I warn him.

"Like what?"

"Like you're undressing me with your eyes."

Charlie looks at me innocently, a smug smile on his face. "I don't know what you're talking about."

It's not lost on me how extraordinarily handsome he looks tonight. He undoes the buttons on his wrists and rolls the sleeves up, exposing his muscular arms. I hadn't really noticed before how chiseled he is.

Or rather, I didn't *let* myself notice.

Either way, I'm noticing now.

I lose myself in looking at the menu before my face gives my thoughts away. I bite the corner of my lip as I imagine those tan arms sliding along my skin—

"Beth Ann," he repeats.

"Yes?" I ask breathlessly, shaking my head to get rid of the fantasy within. I feel the flush creep down my neck.

Charlie cocks his head slightly and smirks as he narrows his eyes.

"White wine or red?" Our waitress asks. I hadn't even noticed her arrival.

"Red is fine," I say, blinking rapidly.

The waitress nods and says she'll be back with our drinks in just a moment.

I settle in my chair and look at Charlie. "What are we even supposed to talk about? We've known each other for so long, I mean, we know everything about each other."

He leans back in his chair, settling his elbows on the armrests. "I guess that means we're free to talk about anything. You nervous, Beth Ann?"

"Maybe a little," I admit.

Our waitress returns with two glasses of red wine, breadsticks, and salad. She arranges the table nicely before disappearing again.

Charlie raises his glass in a toast and I do the same.

"To old friendship and a new beginning," he says. I echo him and we clink the glasses together. I'd forgotten how good the wine is at Regiano's. I don't get over here often, but it's a nice treat every now and then.

Through salads and entrees, we rehash the glory days, laughing over inside jokes and the woes of being broke college kids. The wine flows as easily as the conversation does, making me feel as light as a feather. Charlie and I laugh and laugh; edging into something more than just friends. It's so much easier than I thought it would be.

*Why did I fight this for so long?*

He orders a piece of Italian creme cake for us to share. Our forks scrape against the china plate and we take turns devouring it. I make a mental note to ask Thea to add it to her menu of baked goods at the diner.

"You can have the last bite," he says.

I shake my head. "I'm okay. You can have it."

"No, you."

"Fine." I swipe my fork at the last bite of cake and scoop it into my mouth with a smile. I can feel the smear of icing at the corner of my lips, but before I can lift my napkin, Charlie reaches across the table and wipes it off with his thumb. He doesn't break eye contact as he brings it to his mouth and licks it clean.

My breath catches in my throat.

Other couples disappear from the patio one by one until we're the only table left. I recognize the song that has just started playing softly on the radio overhead and I start swaying in my seat to the melody. Charlie smiles as he watches me before standing up and holding out his hand.

"May I have this dance?" he asks.

I stare up at him for a moment before deciding to let go of my inhibitions.

I stand and offer my hand to him. He grasps it and I notice how perfectly they fit together. He pulls me in close enough that I can smell his cologne again. I breathe him in; his scent and the wine in my system making me dizzy.

His other hand returns to the small of my back as we dance. We sway wordlessly under the twinkling lights. I don't want anything to disrupt this moment and I don't trust myself to not say something stupid.

My cheeks are flushed from the alcohol and I lean my head against his chest as we dance. I hear his heartbeat and for the first time in my life, I realize that home isn't a place — it's a person. Charlie's been my home for years now, it just took me a long time to find my way there.

The song ends too quickly, but we don't stop. We keep swaying as another one comes on, and another after that. It's only when our waitress returns to the patio, looking perturbed, that we finally return to the table.

Charlie throws a hundred dollar bill down on the table and tells her to keep the change, all the while still holding onto my hand. We stagger through the restaurant like giddy teenagers. He's pulling me toward the door as I notice we are the last couple remaining. They must have been waiting on us to leave so they could close. A wave of guilt washes over me; I know exactly what that's like.

"Sorry!" I yell over my shoulder as we exit. I giggle as we make our way back to our cars, digging around in my clutch for my keys.

"Oh, no," Charlie says, reaching for my hand. "You're not driving. You've had too much wine."

"Did you get me drunk on purpose?" I ask playfully.

"Let me take you home," he whispers as he brushes hair away from my face.

He looks at my lips and I sober up a bit, thinking he's going to kiss me again. He smiles as he takes ahold of my hand and walks around to the passenger side of his SUV and opens the door. He helps me in and then shuts it behind me before walking over to his side.

We hold hands all the way back to my house. Granted, it's a short drive, but it's a large step for us.

Charlie walks me up the porch steps like he's done so many times before, but the air between us is different this time. It's charged with possibility.

I thank my lucky stars that Thea is out of the house tonight.

I fumble with the key in the lock, not wanting to let go of his hand. Our fingers are still intertwined as I finally get it open. I turn around in the doorway and stare up at him as the stars twinkle overhead and waves crash in the distance.

"I had a really great time tonight," I begin, my voice no louder than a whisper.

Charlie smiles. Then, as if in slow motion, he leans down and presses his lips to mine. It's different than when we kissed this morning in the parking lot. That was quick and new, this is tender and passionate.

He kisses me gently in the moonlight. His hands cradle my face delicately between them.

I bite my lip when we separate and stare at him, searching his eyes. Maybe it's the wine or maybe it's Charlie, but every nerve ending inside of me is on fire and I feel like I might combust on the spot.

"I did, too," he says, his voice dripping with desire.

I can't help myself. I rise up on my tiptoes and kiss him again, balling my fists into his shirt to pull him closer to me. I want him closer; I'd crawl into his skin if I could.

We part; years of pent-up emotions break free, igniting a hunger in him that I've never seen before.

We barely make it through the doorway before his lips are back on mine. Charlie kicks the door shut. I'm walking backwards through the hallway and hit my hip on the table. It reminds me of a day in the diner when I'd done the same thing going to see Judith.

Judith.

I banish thoughts of her from my memory, focusing on the man in front of me. The pain in my hip is nothing compared to the desire in my heart.

He has me pressed against the wall and his hands are at the base of my neck now, tangled in my hair. He gives a quick tug and I lean back under his command, baring my neck to him.

"Good girl," he murmurs as he presses a trail of kisses down my throat until he reaches my collarbone and I feel his teeth graze the skin there. "You are more lovely than the stars."

"Charlie," I say. It comes out a half-whisper, not because I want him to stop, but because I want to make sure we both want this. I want to make sure we won't regret this in the morning.

He pauses and looks at me; his face illuminated by the pale moonlight streaming in through the window in the door. I search his eyes.

"Are you sure?" I ask through a trembling breath.

"I've never been so sure of anything in my entire life," he replies. "Are *you* sure? This is a line we can't uncross."

"Yes." It comes out louder and more forceful than I anticipated and he laughs.

"I don't want you to regret this in the morning," he adds, brushing hair out of my face.

"Can't regret something you've waited this long for."

His lips come crashing down on mine again. His hands are at my back, finding the zipper of my dress. Goosebumps spread across my skin like wildfire as he unzips me and begins to slide my dress sleeves off one shoulder at a time.

My phone starts ringing. I frown, distracted now. I start fumbling for my clutch to grab my phone.

"Leave it," he says breathlessly in between kisses on my shoulder.

"I can't, it's Thea," I say, pulling my phone out of my clutch. I blink a few times to get my eyes to focus. Charlie is fighting with my bra straps as I answer.

"Hello?"

Instead of Thea's voice, I'm met with Raquel's. "Hi!" she says.

"Raquel, what is going on?" I ask, eager to end this conversation and get back to kissing Charlie.

"Um, okay." Her voice is higher than normal and I know instantly that something is wrong. "We came out with some of my friends to Ramona's and I think someone spiked Thea's drink."

"What?" Everything around me stops and time stands still. Charlie freezes, staring at me intently.

“I know what you’re thinking,” Raquel says, “but she was being good and just drinking a soda, not alcohol. She’s acting really weird and I called an ambulance.”

“Oh my God, where are you?” I can hear sirens in the distance but can’t tell if they’re coming from outside the house or through the phone. It has Charlie’s attention now, too. Hastily, he slides my dress sleeves back onto my shoulders and spins me around, zipping me up.

“The ambulance is almost here, just meet us at the hospital,” Raquel says before she hangs up.

“Oh my God,” I repeat as I face Charlie again.

“What is it?” he asks. Concern laces his face.

“It’s Thea,” I say slowly. “Someone spiked her drink.”

# Chapter Twelve

## Thea

Raquel and I are having a sleepover tonight while Aunt Beth has a long overdue date night with Charlie. Her house is just a couple of blocks away from ours, so I make the short trek through the neighborhood. I sling my duffle bag over my shoulder and it swings into my side as I make my way to Raquel's.

The warm air wraps around me as I walk. There's a strong breeze tonight and my hair whips around my face. I repeat her directions over and over again as I walk.

*Take a left at the blue mailbox, and then a right after two blocks.*

I walk up to a small, olive green cottage. It shines like a beacon of eccentricity on a street lined with white and beige-toned houses. So, of course it belongs to Raquel.

There is barely enough room to climb the porch steps due to the overwhelming number of potted plants and succulents. I'm careful to avoid knocking any over as I cross the tiny porch. I knock on the door and hear her yell from inside.

"It's open!"

I let myself in and am immediately engulfed by the comforting scent of cinnamon. Her home is warm and inviting, painted in jewel tones, and seemingly decorated by someone's hippie grandma. There's a shoe rack next to the door, so I slip off my flip-flops before going any further.

"Hey," she says, rounding the corner from the living room. She's got a royal blue tank top on and the color pops against her pale, freckled skin.

"Hi," I say. "Happy birthday!"

"Thank you." She grins. "Give me ten minutes to change and then we can go."

"Take your time," I tell her. "We've got all night."

"True. Do you want a tour?" she asks.

"Sure!"

She motions for me to follow her and I do. We walk into the living room. It's vastly different from the one at Beth's house. Raquel's is colorful; the walls are painted a deep, royal purple and there's wind-chimes in the corner by the window. Her furniture is mismatched, but full of character. Her sofa is olive green corduroy, and there's a dark leather chair caddy-cornered to it. A small coffee table sits in front of the couch, a rainbow mosaic covering its top.

She shows me the living room, a small kitchen, her bathroom and bedroom, and stops when she nears another bedroom.

"Uh, this is my studio," she says quietly as she opens the door.

Behind it is an artist's dream space. Big windows overlook her small backyard and let in tons of natural light. There's a desk in the corner, and an easel in the center of the room.

"Wow," I breathe as I step into the room. Artwork lines the walls and I'm astonished by it. Nature scenes, abstract pieces, and portraits are scattered along the wall. "You never told me you are an artist!"

"I dabble," she says, her cheeks turning red, just like that first day in the diner. "Right now, I'm working with watercolors."

I glance at the easel and her current creation, a sailboat on the sea at sunset.

"This would look fantastic at the diner. You're really talented," I say.

"Thanks," Raquel says. "I don't tell many people about it."

"Why not? You should!"

She shrugs. "I get a little embarrassed."

I turn to look at her. "This is nothing to be embarrassed about. I wish I could do this!"

"We could paint together sometime," she says, "I could teach you."

"I'd like that." I feel the grin on my face growing wider as I turn back to look at her.

"Oh my gosh, Penny could join us! We could have a girls craft club or something!"

I nod enthusiastically. "That sounds fantastic."

Raquel steps out of her studio after a few moments and I follow suit. She shuts the door behind her and we return to her bedroom. I sit down on her bed while she ventures into her closet to change.

Her bed feels like a giant marshmallow and I sink into it with a contented sigh. A giant, fluffy orange cat jumps up on the bed next to me.

"Hello," I say to it.

Raquel pops her head out of the closet and smiles. "That's Mr. Miles," she says before ducking back into her clothes.

"Hello," I repeat, "Mr. Miles." I offer my hand out to the cat and he rubs against it, purring affectionately.

"What do we think about this?" Raquel asks as she steps out in front of me. She's in shorts and a black sequined top. It reminds me of Judith.

"Too fancy?" she asks.

I shrug. "It's your birthday dinner."

"I just don't know if this is the vibe I want to go for," she says, before spinning around to look at her reflection in the full-length mirror in the corner. She ponders it for a moment and then parades back into her closet. I hear hangers scrape as she moves them along.

She steps back out in a light blue top a few moments later. It's floral print and makes her skin look sun-kissed.

"There it is," I say as I pet Mr. Miles. "That's the one."

She glances at her reflection in the mirror again and seems content with what she sees. She grabs some earrings off her dresser and sticks them in before grabbing a small, black purse.

"Ready?" she asks.

"Sure." I give Mr. Miles one last pat before I stand up and follow her out. She turns the light off and walks down the hallway, an extra pep in her step. Raquel grabs her keys off of a hook by the front door and I follow her back out onto the porch. She locks the door behind me and we walk down the front steps single file to avoid all the potted plants.

Panic starts to rise in my chest at the thought of riding in her car, but I fight it. I take a deep breath in through my nostrils and remind myself that I'm okay. I am stronger than this fear. I think of a technique mentioned in one of the pamphlets Amber gave me — breathe in for four seconds, hold for seven, and exhale for eight.

I open the car door as I exhale and sit down in the passenger seat. Raquel puts her key in the ignition and turns it; the car roars to life. The radio starts blaring and she quickly turns it down.

"Sorry," she says, messing with the knob. "I like to jam out sometimes."

"It's fine," I laugh, imagining her rocking out on the way to work.

She backs out of her driveway and begins to tell me about who all will be joining us for her birthday celebration. I nod and pretend to listen, more focused on keeping myself sane. I take another deep breath in.

*One, two, three, four.*

"Penny had a family emergency," Raquel says, "otherwise, she would be joining us."

"Bummer," I mutter. "I hope everything's okay."

"I invited Graham, but he said he was helping his mom make more of her salsa. Said the festival really wiped her out."

I smile, thinking of him spending time with his sweet mother.

"I booked the party room at Ramona's Pizzeria, but we probably could have gotten away with just a big table," she says. "It won't be a huge crowd."

I nod and focus on my breathing. Ramona's is Beth's favorite pizza place and I make a mental note to take home a pizza for her.

We drive across Driftbay with the windows rolled down, letting the warm summer air blow through our hair. The sensation feels good on my skin and helps to ground me. Raquel fiddles with the stereo volume as she drives; favorite songs keep playing.

We pull into Ramona's a little past eight. Beth and Charlie should just be starting their date and I can't help but wonder how it's going.

Ramona's is a small place, similar in style to the tavern that Jake took me to. The exterior is painted white, just like the tavern, but has red lettering along the front. Judging from experience, I'm finding that the hole-in-the-wall places have the best food.

Raquel parks and shuts off the car. We get out and she excitedly takes off across the gravel parking lot and greets some of her other friends. I tag along behind her and catch up to the group. She introduces me to them, but I quickly forget their names. I'm still on edge from being in the car and doing my best to keep calm.

I follow them into the restaurant and towards the back party room, my nose filling with the scent of Italian spices and marinara sauce. It makes my stomach grumble. This place looks like it hasn't been remodeled since the 90's, with its dingy gray carpet and red, stained glass lamps over every table. It's charming, if only because it feels comfortable and nostalgic.

Raquel takes her spot at the head of the table and I take a seat next to her. She is animated as she talks to some friends from college that stuck around town; I focus more on the menu in front of me. I'm debating between a plain cheese pizza or pepperoni when our waitress comes by to take drink orders.

Everyone rattles off what they'd like. Raquel orders a water and then it's my turn. I quickly order a Dr. Pepper and then the many conversations are back in full force. I tune them out and study the menu some more, as if it's the most interesting thing I've ever read. Everyone seems to know each other, except for me.

"You okay?" Raquel asks quietly.

"Yeah." I nod. "Just a little overwhelmed, but I'll be okay."

Our drinks arrive and we place our food orders. Raquel orders a pie with anchovies on it. I don't know how she stomachs them. I order a plain cheese pizza and hand my menu back to our waitress.

"Did Raquel ever tell you about the time I was asleep and she did my makeup and painted my toenails?"

I look up and meet the gaze of the man sitting across from me. I think it's her brother, Blake.

"No," I laugh.

"Why would I have told her that?" Raquel asks, laughing.

He shrugs. "It's a funny story," he says. He looks back at me and takes a sip of his drink before launching into the tale.

"So, I would have been around eleven at the time, and Raquel, you were what? Eight?"

She nods. "Sounds about right."

"Anyways, I had this big basketball game one Saturday morning. Our mom was away for work so our dad was in charge of us all weekend. Raquel thought it would be hilarious to sneak into my room that morning and draw all over my face with Mom's lipstick and eyeliner. And boy, that stuff stained, let me tell you."

I laugh, thinking of a younger version of Raquel, ever the artist, utilizing her mediums.

"Don't forget, I painted your fingernails *and* toenails, too," she says.

"How could I? They were hot pink and glittery! The guys gave me so much crap after that game."

She snickers as he continues.

"Of course, I didn't get up early enough to take it off, I was doing good just to get the makeup washed off. She drew a fake mustache on me and colored in my eyebrows with the eyeliner. I looked like a crazy person."

"Well, you were," Raquel says, nudging her brother's shoulder.

"I almost busted her bedroom door down when I realized what she'd done," Blake says. "Dad was so pissed and already at his wit's end without Mom being home."

"Being grounded was so worth it," Raquel says, "seeing you play the championship game with hot pink, sparkly fingernails was the icing on top."

"I still think those sparkles are what won us that game," he says. "They blinded the other team."

Raquel laughs loudly at those words.

"Do you have any siblings?" Blake asks me.

I shuffle in my seat. "Nope," I say, "I'm an only child."

"Bummer," he says. He looks back at Raquel and adds, "We may have gotten on each other's nerves when we were kids, but I don't know what I'd do without my baby sis." He grabs his glass and raises it, picking up his fork from the table. He dings it against the glass, getting everyone's attention.

"To the birthday girl," he says, in a toast, "to know you is to love you and I hope you have the best birthday possible."

Everyone raises their glass and murmurs words of affection back to Raquel before taking a drink.

It isn't long before the pizzas come out and conversation dies down. Everyone starts eating, mingling and laughing through bites of pizza and salad. Our waitress is working her butt off making sure everyone has refills and everything they need.

Once all of the dishes and empty cups have been cleared from the table, and stories of yesteryear discussed, Blake excuses himself. A few moments later, he returns with a cake for the birthday girl and places it in front of her. It's tall, definitely a double-layer cake, covered in chocolate icing. He pulls a lighter out of his pocket and flicks it on, proceeding to light the candles on the cake. We all start singing to Raquel and cheer as she blows out the candles.

Blake disappears in search of more plates and a knife so we can cut the cake. I feel assaulted from all sides by the numerous conversations happening around me. Stories of Raquel from college, previous jobs, childhood friends, and so on. I just need a moment to myself to breathe.

No one pays any attention to me as I exit the party room. I walk over to the bar area and breathe a sigh of relief. It's shockingly quiet here compared to the party room.

The bartender strides over to me as I sit down on a barstool. He's tall, bearded, and dressed in a white band T-shirt that looks like it's from the 80's.

"What can I get you?" he asks.

"Actually, just a Dr. Pepper, if possible," I say with a laugh. I play with my necklace, turning the stone over between my fingers. "I feel bad asking our waitress for another; she's working her butt off."

He laughs. "Coming right up."

I stare at the alcohol bottles lining the shelves behind the bar. Part of me wants to experience that mind-numbing bliss again, but another part worries about disappointing Beth again. Though more so, I want to make Beth and now Amber proud of me.

He places my soda down in front of me and I bring the glass to my lips. The carbonation burns my nose as I take a sip.

"Hey."

Raquel settles onto the barstool beside me. "You okay?" she asks.

"Yeah, it was just really loud and overwhelming in there," I nod back toward the party room. "Just needed a minute."

Raquel opens her mouth to say something but is interrupted when we hear my name shouted across the room.

"Thea!"

I swivel on the barstool to see Jake making his way up to the bar.

"Oh, brother," I groan as I roll my eyes.

"Did you talk to Emily at the festival the other day?" he asks. Fury burns in his green eyes.

"Yeah," I answer, a bit hesitantly.

"She dumped me."

"And that's her problem, how?" Raquel asks.

"She said *you* talked to her," he huffs as he points at me. "I told you, my dad can ruin anyone in this town and that's sland-"

"Oh, *enough* with your dad," I snap, feeling bold. "If you don't want me to say bad things about you, then you shouldn't do bad things."

Raquel snorts beside me.

"And just what are you laughing at?" he demands.

"Tiny man syndrome," she says, holding her thumb and index finger barely apart. She giggles even harder now.

I don't hide the laugh that bubbles out of my chest.

"You'll regret this," he says.

" Jake, go find someone else to annoy," I say, waving him away.

He opens his mouth to say something else but is distracted by a crash from across the restaurant. Raquel and I turn in the direction of the noise to see a waitress attempting to clean up two pizzas she'd dropped.

"Just remember, what goes around, comes around," Jake says, bringing the attention back to him.

We swivel back on our barstools to face him. I sense a change in his demeanor. He seems calmer.

"Okay," I say. "Whatever."

"Buh-bye," Raquel says to him, making a grand motion of waving. I take another sip of my soda.

Jake turns on his heels and barrels past another couple walking into the bar area as he heads for the front door.

"God, he is such a jerk," I say as I turn back to Raquel. "I can't believe I went out with him."

"Yeah, even after I tried to warn you," she says. "Though, I probably could have tried harder."

I pick up my soda and take another drink. "At least Graham showed up that night. Kind of like a knight in shining armor. Or, rather, surfer on a golf cart."

Raquel lets out a belly laugh at that. "Sorry," she says, quieting herself down.

"Your brother seems nice," I tell her.

"Yeah, I'm glad I have him. We fought like cats and dogs growing up, but we have a new understanding and appreciation for each other now."

We sit in silence for a few moments.

"Is this everything you imagined and more for a birthday dinner?" I ask her as I finish my drink. The bartender swoops up the empty glass and gently tosses it behind the counter.

She nods. "If only Graham and Penny were here, too," she says. "You haven't had any cake yet! It's amazing, you have to at least try it. You want to go back?" She points behind her to the party room.

"Sure," I say, with a frown. Everything looks a little fuzzy around the edges, like when you're so tired that your eyes can't focus. I blink a few times trying to clear my vision but that only seems to make things worse. The room feels like it's spinning around me.

"You okay?" Raquel asks.

"Yeah," I reply. "I think I just turned my head too fast." I reach up and rub my temples.

"I hate when I do that."

I shake my head as if to shake the feeling away, but it doesn't subside. I close my eyes, but that only makes the spinning sensation worse. It's starting to feel like I'm on a cheap fair ride, being thrown around and around again.

"Thea?" Raquel's voice sounds distant now.

I grip the edge of the bar and try to stand, hoping to steady the whirling inside my mind.

"Thea, are you okay?"

My limbs feel disconnected from my body and the floor seems to ripple beneath me.

My foot doesn't find solid ground and I tumble off of the barstool. My head hits the concrete floor; searing pain cuts through the whirling chaos in my skull. I hear Raquel call my name once more and then everything goes dark.

# Chapter Thirteen

## Beth

We're out of the house and back in Charlie's SUV in a flash. He drives across town to the hospital wordlessly, but keeps a firm grip on my hand the entire time.

I shake my head as we drive. "I don't know how to parent her," I admit.

"Hey," Charlie says as he rubs my knuckles comfortingly. "She wasn't drinking again. Raquel said she had a soda. That's a good thing."

"I shouldn't have let her go out." I rest my head against the back of the seat and let it loll to the side to look at him.

"That isn't your fault, either." He glances at me. "Really, Beth Ann, it's not. She's an adult, you have to give her a little freedom."

I shake my head, feeling the guilt wash over me.

"She's going to be okay. I've seen this a couple of times. She'll have a rough day or so, but she'll be okay."

It doesn't make me feel better. I just want to be able to protect her.

Charlie pulls over to the side of the road, seeing flashing lights behind us. The ambulance flies by us and he switches lanes to follow behind it. We pull into the hospital parking lot and I can't believe how much has changed since we met here mere hours ago. He stops long enough for me to jump out of the vehicle as Thea is being unloaded from the back of the ambulance. He speeds off to find a parking spot.

I take a few steps toward her but am stopped when an EMT slams their arm out in front of me.

"Ma'am, you can't go any further," he tells me.

"That's my niece," I say.

"I understand, but ma'am, you can't go further."

It's then that I notice Raquel climbing out of the back of the ambulance, holding a cup of dark liquid.

"Beth," she says frantically. She hands the cup off to another paramedic and he disappears into the hospital.

"I swear she was drinking soda," she insists as she joins my side.

I shake my head. At this point, I don't care. I just want Thea to be okay.

"Tell me what happened," I say as I lead her away from the ambulance and toward the emergency room entrance.

"She was fine and then started complaining she was dizzy. She tried to get up off the barstool and collapsed. She hit her head and wouldn't respond to anything."

Charlie comes running up to join us, having parked the car. He ushers the two of us through the automatic doors. We are greeted by a calm receptionist who directs us to the waiting room. I take a seat on the plastic-covered chair between Charlie and Raquel and nervously begin to tap my foot, the sharp clicking of my high-heel filling the room. Charlie places a hand on my thigh; his touch instantly soothing my frayed nerves. Raquel notices but doesn't say anything.

We wait.

And wait.

And wait some more.

I find comfort in resting my head on Charlie's shoulder as we sit there. Finally, I look over at Raquel.

"You don't have to stay," I say quietly, so as to not disturb the other people in the waiting room.

"I want to." She looks tired but becomes a bit more animated when she starts talking. "She's my friend and I want to make sure she's okay. Besides, it was my fault we were out tonight anyways."

Charlie stands up to stretch his legs and once he makes sure I'm okay for the moment, announces he's going on a short walk. I nod and turn back to Raquel.

"Can you think of anyone who might have done this? Or anyone you recognized in the bar?"

"We saw Jake in the bar," she says, "He was mad about her talking to some girl named Emily. He was pretty pissed off and then all of a sudden, he wasn't."

My blood boils as I think about Jake, the way he treated Thea, and the possibility of him doing this. I make a mental note to tell Charlie so it can be investigated later.

He returns a few moments later with three bottles of water and some snacks from the vending machine. He passes a pack of snack crackers to me and one to Raquel.

"Oh," I say, holding my hand up. "I'm not hung-"

"Eat," he commands. "You had a lot of wine." He's in official sheriff mode.

Begrudgingly, I take the crackers and open them before cracking open the water bottle. My stomach grumbles in appreciation.

Raquel opens hers and quietly nibbles on the crackers, all the while staring at the tile floor.

"I shouldn't have taken her," she says quietly.

Charlie looks at her. "This is not your fault, Raquel. Both of you listen to me. This is not your fault."

She nods as if she understands. "I just feel so bad." She puts her head in her hands.

A doctor, clad in a long white coat, walks into the waiting room.

"I'm looking for the family of Thea Calloway," he announces as he looks around the room.

We three stand.

He acknowledges us with a nod and motions for us to follow him. We scurry across the waiting room after him, as he leads us to a small, private room. He steps behind the desk and Charlie motions for Raquel and I to sit in the chairs.

The clock on the wall tells me that it's well past two in the morning.

"I'm Dr. Kwapis. We found rohypnol, a common date-rape drug, in Thea's system," he says. "It matched the sample from the drink that came in with her." He looks between us. "Which one of you brought it in?"

Raquel raises her hand.

"Good. Thank you." He offers her a comforting smile and then turns to me. "Your daughter's friend's quick-thinking really helped us figure out what was going on."

I don't correct him on the terminology of what Thea is to me.

"Is she okay?" I ask.

"We had to pump her stomach to get the drug out of her system, but yes, she is okay. I'd like to keep her until the morning, at least, for observation. She's going to feel sick for another day or two, but I expect she will make a full recovery."

I let out a deep breath and feel Charlie's hand rest reassuringly on my shoulder.

"She's awake now, but groggy, if you'd like to see her."

I nod and stand, following Dr. Kwapis out of the room. Raquel and Charlie tag along behind us as we venture through the emergency room and down a hallway. They stay outside her room as Dr. Kwapis leads me inside.

Thea is in the hospital bed, hooked up to monitors and wearing an oxygen mask. I grab the seat to her right and quietly pull it up next to the bed. I take her hand in mine and sit there quietly, running my thumb over her knuckles. I listen to the sound of her breathing for a few moments.

Thea stirs and opens her eyes. "Aunt Beth," she says as she sees me, "what happened?"

Tears spring to my eyes at the sound of her voice. I've been so focused on not losing Charlie as my best friend that I didn't realize just how close I had been to losing Thea.

"You were out with Raquel," I begin, struggling to keep my voice even around the lump in my throat, "and someone spiked your drink."

Terror flashes in her eyes.

"I wasn't drinking, Aunt Beth," she starts, "I swear I wasn't drinking."

"Shhh, baby," I comfort her, giving her a smile and calling her a nickname I haven't called her since she was ten. "I know. It's okay. You're going to be okay."

She stares at me. "I'm so tired."

"Rest." I stroke her forehead, my fingers grazing her hairline. "Just rest. Don't worry about anything else, okay?"

The door opens and Charlie steps in, quickly closing it behind him.

"How is she?" he whispers.

"Groggy," I say, looking back at Thea. Her eyes are closed again and she's breathing peacefully.

"They're going to admit her," he says. "I overheard the nurses talking. Just long enough to make sure her vitals stay strong."

I nod. It's going to be a long night.

I sit with Thea for a little while longer before Raquel slips into the room for her turn. Thea stirs in the bed but is awake enough now to talk to her for a little bit.

Charlie and I let them have their space, stepping out of the room.

"Why don't you come back to my place," he says, looping our hands together. He lives a block from the hospital. "Get a hot shower and rest until they discharge her. I can bring you back in the morning."

I look at him, grateful for the man that's been placed in my life. Whether as a best friend or something more, he's always been the voice of reason for me.

"Okay." There's no use in arguing. My car is at Regiano's, and my house is on the opposite side of Driftbay; it makes sense to just crash with him.

"They won't let us stay all night, especially once she gets admitted."

"You're right," I say. Visiting hours ended hours ago. "Let me go tell her." I undo my hand from his and step back into the room. Thea is laughing a little at something Raquel has said and I'm glad to see her in brighter spirits.

"I don't mean to break up the party," I begin, "but they're kicking us out soon."

Raquel glances at the watch on her wrist. "Oh, my," she says, noting the time.

I look at Thea. "I'm going to go to Charlie's and get a couple hours of sleep and then I'll be back to get you, okay?"

She nods.

"I love you," I add.

"I love you, too," she says, slumber lacing her voice.

Raquel stands and walks across the room to my side. "You scared me, Thea," she says, a smile slowly spreading across her face.

Thea doesn't respond, having already drifted back off to sleep.

Raquel and I quietly exit the room, joining Charlie in the hallway. I glance around and see a blonde-headed nurse at the desk and walk towards her.

"Hi," I say, getting her attention. She looks up at me with a doe-eyed expression.

"Hello," she says cheerfully. I wish I had her energy.

"I'm Thea Calloway's aunt and I wanted to leave my phone number just in case."

"Oh my God," she breathes as she looks at me. She shakes her head. "You're Beth of Beth Ann's Diner, right?"

I smile and nod. "Yes."

"Your cinnamon roll snickerdoodles got me through my breakup earlier this year." She hands me a sticky note and a pen. "They were out of this world."

"Thank you." I scribble my phone number on the piece of paper and hand it back to her.

She looks at Charlie now. "Hi, Sheriff Gajewski," she says.

Charlie puts his hands in his pockets. "Hi, Hannah."

Hannah directs us on how to exit the emergency room and we head out. Charlie puts his arm around my shoulders as we walk.

"Didn't realize I was with a local celebrity tonight," he says.

I playfully slap his side. "Oh, stop it."

Raquel laughs from behind us and for a moment, I'd forgotten she was there.

Charlie and I break apart as we stand in the glow of the emergency room entrance.

"Raquel, do you need a ride home?" he asks. He always thinks of everything and everyone.

"Actually, if you could drive me back to Ramona's to get my car," she says, "that would be great."

He nods. "Wait here and I'll get the car."

Charlie takes off across the parking lot. We watch as he gets in it and starts the engine, then whips around to the entrance to pick us up.

I climb into the front passenger seat while Raquel clambers around in the back. It's a wordless drive as we take off in the direction of the bar. I pull out my phone and send a group text to my staff that due to a family emergency, the diner will not be open today. Thea is more important than the diner and besides, a portion of the staff was involved in the emergency.

My eyes keep fluttering closed as Charlie drives. I lean my head against the window, just wanting to sleep. I'm exhausted from the night's events, both physically and emotionally. It's been a whirlwind.

We drop Raquel off and say our goodbyes. Then Charlie drives us back across town to his apartment. There's no traffic at four-thirty in the morning.

The exhaustion is deep in my bones by the time we get out of the car. My legs feel like they have lead in them. He takes my hand and leads me through the entrance and up a staircase to his second-floor bachelor pad.

"Stay here," he instructs me as I stand in his living room. I glance around the room. Framed photographs of his family line the mantle and adorn the coffee table. He returns a moment later with a pair of sweatpants and a T-shirt for me.

"Towels and washcloths are in the bathroom closet. Sorry, but I don't have any frilly-smelling shampoo or anything."

I start to giggle. I don't know if what he just said was actually funny or if I'm *that* tired.

"You can have the bed," he says as he leads me toward the master bedroom.

"What about you?" I ask.

"I'm good on the couch."

I open my mouth to protest but he's already fighting me.

"Really, Beth Ann. Give me a blanket and a pillow and I'm fine."

I don't argue with him anymore; I just want to get out of this dress and these damn heels. I close the door to the bathroom and kick them off. My feet ache with relief at being on level ground again. I take the earrings out of my earlobes and lay them on the counter. After grabbing a towel and washcloth, I turn on the hot water and with some struggle, unzip my dress and strip it off. I leave my belongings in a pile on the floor and step into the shower.

The tension starts to leave my body as the hot water pounds my back. I wet my hair and reach down for the shampoo, laughing to myself over the names of men's products. My options are Ocean, Mahogany Teakwood, and Noir...whatever the hell those are supposed to smell like. I sniff each of them and go for the one that smells the most like him.

I quickly finish my shower and get out, towel-drying my hair. I throw on the sweatpants and one of his old Driftbay Police Department shirts. I feel like a zombie as I head to the bed and collapse in it.

The mattress is like a marshmallow and I think I could fall asleep in seconds. I force my eyes open and stare at the ceiling fan for a moment before I get back up. Something is missing.

I march out to the living room where Charlie is making a cot on the couch, standing there in a gray T-shirt and boxers.

"Get in the bed," I say.

"What?" he asks, looking up at me.

"Get in the bed," I repeat. "We've both had a long night and deserve good rest."

Charlie smiles.

"No funny stuff, though, I mean it."

He holds up his fingers in a scout's honor symbol. "Of course not," he says.

He abandons his cot and follows me into his bedroom.

"I normally sleep on the left," he says.

"Well, that's great, because I normally take the right." I smile. It's nice to be in-sync with him for once.

I glance at the alarm clock as I lie down — I guess two and a half hours of sleep are better than none.

I take a deep breath in; everything smells like him. I am surrounded by the scent of Charlie and it's overwhelming yet comforting at the same time.

He turns over and props himself up on his elbow and pillow.

"Is this okay?" he asks as he gently puts an arm around my waist and pulls me closer.

"Yeah," I say, feeling his warmth wrap around me. "This is good. Though you should know, I don't typically sleep with someone on the first date."

I can hear the smile in his voice as I settle against this chest.

"Must be a pretty special guy, then," he says, nuzzling my shoulder.

I smirk, finally allowing myself to fully relax in his embrace, and we drift off to sleep.

I wake up a couple of hours later still wrapped up in Charlie's arms. Sunlight is streaming in through the curtains and for a moment, I just stare at him. Drink him in. Memorize every single line and crevice of his face. I reach out, gently stroking my fingertips along his cheek and jawline, feeling the stubble that has appeared overnight.

Is this a taste of what I have deprived myself of for years? Of this very moment and so many others of domestic bliss?

The last touch is one too many; Charlie stirs and starts to turn over. Except he can't, because I'm entangled in his arms.

He wakes up slowly and blinks a few times as I come into focus. He looks at me like he can't believe this is real.

"Morning," I whisper.

"Good morning."

His right hand is resting on my hip. My shirt has ridden up during the night so he's touching my bare skin. He starts rubbing small circles on the skin beneath his fingertips.

I offer a soft smile as I look at him.

"What?" I ask.

"Just making sure this is real," he says.

"Making sure what is real?"

"You, here. In my bed."

I lean forward a smidge and gently kiss his lips, letting him know that yes, this is very real.

"I didn't keep you awake with my snoring?" I ask.

Charlie roars with laughter, reaching up to rub his eyes. "No," he says as he returns his hand to my skin. "But as much as I would like to stay here and continue this," he adds, squeezing my hip, "we need to go."

"I know." It comes out as a sigh. I don't know when we'll get a moment like this again, but Thea needs me. What's a few more hours or days when Charlie and I have been pining for decades?

"I know," he echoes quietly and I know we're on the same page. He looks at me like I'm the most beautiful woman he's ever seen, and I suddenly don't care about morning breath or sleep in my eyes. There's a different, tender kind of love behind his eyes, the kind that's *not* reserved for your best friend.

"Hey," he says softly. "I just...I know you've got a lot going on with Thea right now, but I just want you to know that I'm here for whatever. However you need me. Friend or...something more."

I smile. "Thank you. I appreciate that."

We eventually untangle ourselves and get up to get on with the day. He drops me off at Regiano's to pick up my car from the night before and I run home to freshen up. I change out of his pajamas and into some jeans and another T-shirt before brushing my teeth and combing my hair. I feel like a new human after I'm done.

What a difference a change of clothes and brushed teeth can make for a person.

I'm back at the hospital right around eight, just when visiting hours are set to begin. I'm directed upstairs to Thea's new room and I ride the elevator up a few floors.

She's more awake now but I can tell she's still out of it. She keeps asking what happened. I've been informed that this is normal and she'll continue to ask as her memory gets better.

After an hour or so, she's finally discharged. A nurse comes in to unhook her from the monitors and IV. I help her as she slides back into her clothes from the night before.

"Are you okay?" I ask her when she's dressed.

She nods. She takes a few cautious steps away from the bed and seems to relax a bit.

"Just take me home, Aunt Beth," she says as we walk out of her room.

Now that, I can do.

We spend the rest of the day at the cottage. I let Thea rest and recoup for the majority of the time but I do try to pick her brain to see what she remembers of the night. To my dismay, it's not much. She has a calm day and I check in on her every hour or so as she rests.

I'm just walking out of her bedroom when I hear a knock at the front door. Walking over to it, I glance through the peephole, not expecting any visitors.

It's Charlie.

I open the door and smile as I see him. He's holding a couple pizza boxes.

"Hey," he says. "Wanted to bring you guys dinner." He hands me the warm boxes, Italian spices filling my nostrils.

"Come in," I say, stepping away from the doorway.

He shakes his head. "I don't want to intrude. Besides, not sure if Thea is up for visitors."

He's right.

"Well, thank you," I say. "I really appreciate it."

"We pulled the security footage from Ramona's," he says. "I'm bringing the punk in for questioning myself. We're gonna get him."

"Thank you," I repeat.

Charlie nods and then kisses me, quickly. "You're welcome. I'll check in with you later," he says before turning around. I watch as he walks down the steps of the porch and back to his car, grateful for the man that's been placed in my life.

I close the front door and head back to the kitchen, placing the pizza boxes on the counter. I grab two plates out of the cabinet and turn around as Thea appears in the doorway.

"Charlie?" she asks, nodding at the pizza.

"Yeah," I say. "He figured we could use some dinner."

"I *am* pretty hungry."

"Here." I hand her a plate and she crosses the kitchen. We open the boxes; my favorite supreme pizza and a plain cheese one for her. She picks a few pieces out and drops them on her plate before heading to the table.

"So," she says quietly, "you were right when you said Osborne boys are no good for you. I wish I'd never gotten involved with Jake at all."

"Oh, honey." I sit down beside her at the table. "I should have asked more questions before. If I had known your date was with him, I never would have let you go, and this wouldn't have happened."

"You never did tell me how you know his dad." Thea picks up a slice and takes a bite. "Tell Charlie thank you, by the way."

I smile. "I, uh..." I let out a breath. "I dated his dad for six years."

"You did not." She leans back in her chair, eyes wide.

"I did." I nod. "I was young and naive, and thought it was love. It was before Jake was born."

"Just think, he could be your son," Thea says, letting out a laugh.

"Oh, no. I wouldn't have let that happen. I never wanted kids."

"And now you're stuck with me," she says quietly as her expression turns sour.

"I didn't mean it like that," I say quickly. I reach for her arm. "I love having you out here, Thea. Truly, I do."

She smiles weakly.

"James and I just wanted different things. I thought he would propose and he ended up cheating on me. Multiple times. After that, I gave up on love. It really wrecked me. I went into therapy over him. He was verbally abusive and treated me so poorly, but I didn't realize it for a few years. Hindsight, ya know?"

"Wow," she says quietly, stewing over my words.

"He didn't support the diner. Wanted me to be home at his beck and call."

"Really? But the diner is your dream."

"He doesn't like to see a woman succeed. Or, at least, not this one."

"Maybe you intimidated him," Thea says. "You and Mom are both such strong women."

"Maybe," I say, pondering it. I pause and add, "Your mother hated him."

"I could see that." She's quiet for a moment. "What about Charlie? You never wanted to pursue that?"

I sigh. "I did. But, the timing never worked out. Until now."

"Until now," Thea repeats. "So, I take it your date went well? Despite me ruining it?"

"You did not ruin it," I laugh. "But yes, I think it did."

"You deserve some happiness." She stares at me as she speaks.

"So do you," I say. "Graham's been asking about you."

The corners of her lips turn upward at the mention of Graham's name.

"Graham," she says quietly as she stares at the table, her cheeks getting red.

"He seems sweet on you. How do you feel about him?"

"I think I really like him." She looks up at me. "Like, really like him."

"Maybe you should call him, if you feel up to it. I'm sure he'd love to hear from you."

"Yeah," she says, picking up her slice again. "Maybe I will."

I'm up early the next morning, something I've grown unaccustomed to since Thea started doing all of the baking. I make a cinnamon coffee cake and some chocolate chip cookies for the diner that morning. I'm just plating them up as it's time to open.

I'm not surprised to see that Judith is one of the first customers through the door.

"Morning, dearie," she says as she takes her place at her usual booth.

"Good morning, Judith." I smile and set a coffee mug down on the table for her.

"Missed you yesterday."

Judith is a stickler about routine.

"Yes, there was a slight change in plans yesterday," I say as I sit down opposite her. Her hair is freshly styled and her arms are covered in silver and bejeweled bangles.

"Is everything okay?" she asks.

I nod slowly, replaying the events of the last forty-eight hours. "It is now."

Judith brings the coffee mug to her lips and eyes me over the top of it. "I heard from a little birdie that you and Charlie went on a date."

The real reason she's here. Judith is quite the gossip.

"We did," I reply carefully, a sly smile tugging at the corners of my lips.

"And how was that?" she asks.

"It was...good." Memories flash in my mind of us before we'd gotten the call about Thea. To think about how the night could have ended...

"See? My little plan was all worth it." She smiles over her coffee mug.

"What are you talking about? Your little plan?" I ask. My attention is piqued now. "What do you mean?"

She continues smirking as she sets her mug down.

"Mmm, wouldn't you like to know, dearie?"

"Judith..." I warn.

"Isn't it just...rather funny how right after we started talking about you and Charlie that he got a date?" she asks. "I mean, really, when is the last time you know of that the man went on a date?"

I narrow my eyes as I stare at her. Really, the timing is impeccable. "But—how—"

"Oh, really, dearie. I'm not stupid. I see how you two look at each other. You just needed a push to figure it out yourselves." She chuckles. "I was just...the push."

"Judith, you did not," I say in disbelief.

"Oh, but I did. I found a nice young lady in town and it's amazing what people will do for some quick cash."

"You bribed her?" I yell. I glance around to make sure no one noticed my outburst and then look back at Judith. "Seriously?" I hiss.

"I don't like that word. It was more so...paying for the truth to come out."

I laugh at the thought of her paying someone to go on a date or two with Charlie, just to force us to admit our feelings for one another and get together.

But I guess that was her plan all along.

"But why?" I ask her. Why be so hell-bent on investing time and money into us?

"Because, dearie," she says as she reaches for my hands. "This old heart wanted you two to realize how badly you both wanted each other before it was too late. You just needed a—" she pauses, thinking of the right phrase, "fairy godmother."

And fairy godmother she was.

I hear the ding of the doorbell and we both see Charlie walking in, just as he does every morning.

"You've made your living," she says as she motions around the diner. She looks pointedly at Charlie as she adds, "now go make your life."

# Chapter Fourteen

## Thea

Aunt Beth lets me come back to the diner a week later, once I've been fully cleared by my doctors. I don't remember seeing Jake at the bar that night but Raquel attests to the fact that he was there. The police department got the security footage from the restaurant that night and Aunt Beth told me that Jake was brought in for questioning not long after we got home from the hospital.

It's nice to settle back into my routine of being at the diner and around my friends. Raquel and Penny checked up on me while I was off work, and Graham text me every single day to check in. He's thoughtful that way.

I'm sitting in the break room with Raquel while Penny is out on the floor. It's been a busy morning so far, but there's a lull and we're taking advantage of it.

Graham walks in, holding two plates of steaming breakfast. I catch a whiff and my stomach grumbles. He sets one in front of Raquel — a bagel sandwich, and then sets the other one down for me. My breath catches as I read the words he's written around the plate and on my omelette in ketchup.

"So?" he asks, cocking an eyebrow. "Will you go to dinner with me tonight?"

Raquel is frozen, bagel in hand and her mouth open. They both stare at me, waiting for my answer.

"Absolutely," I say and a smile spreads across Graham's face.

"Told you it was a matter of when and not if," he says, grinning.

I recall our conversation during the Fourth of July festival while eating our pickle pizza.

Raquel sets her sandwich down and squeals with excitement as she grabs for her napkin.

"Graham!" Beth calls out from the kitchen.

He quickly glances behind him and then looks back at me. "I'll pick you up around five tonight, okay?"

"That sounds great." I pick up a fork and stab at the omelette, my stomach growling.

"Oh, this is perfect!" Raquel exclaims after Graham ducks back into the kitchen. She grabs her sandwich again and takes a bite. She chews her bite for a moment before she asks, "What are you going to wear?"

I glance down at my jeans and sneakers, baggy T-shirt, and apron.

"What, is my apron not sexy enough for you?" I ask playfully. I grab the loose ends from the knot holding it to me and swing them at her in my best burlesque move.

She laughs. "You have to look good," she says, "not that you don't now, but this is important. You both deserve some happiness. Besides, we've been waiting for this all summer."

I narrow my eyes. "What do you mean, 'we'?"

"Beth and I," she says as she takes another bite. "He's had it bad for you since day one."

I think about what she's said, replaying every interaction Graham and I have had since we met. I start to get self-conscious about my appearance. I mentally flip through my closet as we sit there, wondering what I can wear and if it will be up to her standards.

"We're both off at three," she continues, "I could come over and help you get ready if you want."

"Sure," I say. I don't want to admit to her that besides the date with Jake — if you can really even call it that — I've never been on a decent first date before. I have no idea what I'm doing.

"Perfect." She smiles. "It's a date."

Raquel and I head back home later that afternoon to start making me over for my first official date with Graham. I sit on my bed, watching as she stands in front of my closet, flipping through item after item.

"No," she repeats as she moves another hanger to the left. "No, no, no." Three more slide along to the discarded section.

At this point, I'm beginning to wonder if I have anything at all that she will deem worthy of such an occasion. It isn't until she is at the back of my closet that I hear her say, "Yes. This..." she turns around, "this will work."

She's holding a pale pink sundress with small roses on it. I'd forgotten that I had it and it honestly reminds me of the wallpaper in the bathroom I share with Beth. She tosses it to me and declares, "I want to see the full visual. Try it on."

I laugh at her dramatics but do as she commands. I trudge down the hallway and close the bathroom door before stripping my work clothes off and sliding the dress over my skin. It's airy and soft, perfect for a late-July evening in Driftbay. I glance over my reflection for a moment before I open the door and walk back to my bedroom.

She smiles as she sees me.

"I love it," she says. "It's perfect. Now." Raquel puts her hands on her hips and glances around my bedroom. "What are you planning to do about your hair? Makeup? Shoes?"

I shrug.

She turns back to my closet and starts surveying the options for footwear.

"What size shoe are you?" she asks as she picks up a pair then sets them back down.

"Nine," I say, resuming my perch on the bed. I fidget with the chain around my necklace, the peridot charm turning into a worry stone.

She turns around and bends down, undoing the sandals on her feet.

"Me, too," she says, "and these would look perfect with that dress. Trade me!" She tosses the sandals to me and I barely catch them. I slip them on and then get up, grabbing a pair of Converse out of the closet to give to her.

She directs me to the bathroom, to help me with my makeup. She carefully applies a touch of eyeliner and directs me on how to properly apply contour and blush. It's like a crash course in the beauty industry by the time she's done with me. She curls my hair, something I never do. By the end of the afternoon, I barely recognize myself, but in a good way. My features are highlighted by the make-up, not overshadowed. My hair flows gently down my shoulders like a waterfall and frames my face nicely.

She steps back into the hallway and smiles as she admires her handiwork.

"You're ready," she says.

"Really?" I ask. I look down at my feet and wish I'd had time for a pedicure.

"Have fun," she says before kissing my cheek, "and I expect to hear about everything!" She lets me go and heads to the front door. She turns back to blow me a kiss and ends up colliding with Beth in the doorway.

Raquel is a hurricane no matter where she is.

"Sorry," Raquel says as she steps around Beth. She offers me a small wave before she dashes out the door.

Beth shuts the door as I walk down the hallway. She slowly turns around and sets the bag of groceries down on the table in the entryway as she takes in the sight of me.

"Thea," she breathes, her lips curling up into a smile. "You look beautiful."

"Thank you." I blush at her compliment. "Graham asked me to dinner tonight."

"So I've heard." She places a hand on her hip. "He talked about it all afternoon after you left."

"Really?" I ask. I find it hard to imagine someone being that excited to take little ole me out to dinner.

"Really." She nods. "Is he coming here or are you meeting him somewhere?"

"He said he'd pick me up here."

She nods again. "Well, I won't keep you." She glances at her watch. "He should be here any minute."

"Is Charlie coming over for dinner?" I ask, nodding at the groceries.

"Yes," she says and I can't help but notice the giddiness in her voice.

Being smitten looks good on her.

"Be safe and have fun. I love you!" she calls out over her shoulder as she heads towards the kitchen.

I laugh as I walk to the doorway, unsure of what to do with myself until Graham arrives. I look at the phone in my hand; it's four fifty-eight.

Two minutes later at exactly five o'clock, Graham rolls into the driveway...on his golf cart.

I meet him outside as he climbs out of it.

"Hi," he says, grinning. There's a bouquet of daisies in his hand.

"Hi," I repeat, eyeing the golf cart suspiciously. I laugh nervously.

"The golf cart," he begins as he walks around it to me. "I remember you saying cars still freak you out after the accident, so I thought it might be better to take you to dinner in this." He hands me the flowers and motions at the golf cart. "Your chariot awaits."

My heart swells at the gesture. I can't believe he remembered that small detail from a conversation weeks ago.

I bring the flowers to my nose and take a breath of their sweet scent as I reach for his outstretched hand.

"Thank you," I say, with a smile.

"You're quite welcome." He takes my hand and leads me to the golf cart and helps me in. I know Beth is watching from the kitchen window but I'm too excited to care.

Graham looks good tonight. He's exceptionally handsome in his dark jeans and light blue polo. He smells freshly showered, his minty aftershave sharp and clean.

He climbs in and starts the engine. It rumbles to life and jerks a bit as he puts it in reverse to back out of Beth's driveway. Graham pulls out onto the main road and we ride along, well under the speed limit. Thoughts of the last time I was in his golf cart surface, but I banish them from my mind. I don't want to think of that disastrous night, not when one so good is within my grasp.

I can't help but laugh each time we get passed by other drivers. He makes a big show of motioning for them to go around us. It's endearing that someone would put this much thought into making sure I am comfortable. For the first time since the accident, my chest doesn't feel heavy being in a moving vehicle.

"So, where are you taking me?" I ask as the warm late-July air whips my hair around my face. I brush a strand behind my ear as I wait for his answer.

"Regiano's," he replies. "I hope you like Italian food." He glances at me and winks.

Notably, the same restaurant that Charlie and Beth had their first date at. It's the fanciest restaurant in town. I've heard it's decent, but not as good as the diner, according to Beth's customers. Though, they might be a tad biased.

We make small talk all the way to Regiano's. Graham parks the golf cart at the back of the restaurant. He jumps off, pocketing the key, and jogs around to my side before I know it. He offers me his hand to help me off and I lay the daisies on the seat. I smooth my hair down as we walk around to the front door. Butterflies dance in my stomach as we hold hands; I can feel my palms getting clammy already.

Regiano's closely resembles Olive Garden, one thing I do miss about Seattle. There aren't many chain restaurants here in Driftbay, just locally-owned places like Beth's.

A hostess clad in all black smiles as she sees us approach.

"Hi!" she says enthusiastically. "Table for two?" She glances at the computer on the station in front of her.

Graham nods, still holding my hand.

"Would you like inside or outside?" she asks.

"Outside," he says.

The hostess nods and leads us through the crowded restaurant and out onto the patio. It's quieter out here and more romantic with fairy lights strung overhead. It was definitely a good idea to come here.

There's a few other couples on the patio, but each are enthralled in their own conversations and don't pay any attention to us. Our hostess seats us at a table in the corner and gives us our menus before she leaves.

I look around in awe, delighted by the decor. It's when I look back at our table that I notice Graham has just been watching me, with a grin on his face.

"What?" I ask, leaning my head onto my palm.

"It's cute watching you discover stuff like this." He gestures around the patio. "Stuff I've seen my whole life and have taken for granted."

"I take it you've been here a time or two then," I say before our waitress approaches. We both order water and then she's on her way again.

"You could say that," Graham says once she's gone. "It was my parents' favorite place. We came here every year for birthdays and anniversaries growing up. It's just...the kind of place where you bring someone special."

I smile at him while he talks. I probably look like a lovesick puppy, but I don't care. It is incredibly sweet that he chose to bring me here when this place is associated with so many happy memories.

"Thank you for bringing me here," I say quietly.

"Of course." He picks up his menu. "Do you want recommendations?"

Our waitress returns with our drinks and complimentary breadsticks and salad. She leaves us again as I start to ponder the menu.

"Recommendations," I say, getting overwhelmed with my choices.

"Alfredo is always a favorite," Graham starts, "my mom loves the lasagna and says it's to die for. My sisters like the ravioli and spaghetti, respectively."

"Who likes which one?" I ask as I look up at him, thinking of when he first told me about Ginny and Betty. "It's important to know their stance on pasta."

He laughs again. "Betty is a big ravioli person. Even the cheap, canned kind. Ever since she was little, she's been all about it. Ginny, on the other hand, is a spaghetti person. It's classic and a staple. Kind of describes her, too."

"And what about you?" I ask as I reach for a breadstick.

"I'm definitely a shrimp Alfredo kind of guy."

I nod my head as I take a bite of bread.

"You?" he asks as he leans across the table.

"Alfredo," I say after I swallow. "Plain and boring, that's me!"

"Thea, you are not boring. In fact, I think you're extraordinary."

I feel my cheeks start to warm and I know it's from his eyes on me and *not* the candle in the middle of the table.

"And how dare you insult the perfection of Alfredo," he teases, reaching for a breadstick. He takes a bite and stares at me. "It's all about mindset. It can be boring if you let it, but I prefer to think of it as dependable. A classic."

"Dependable, huh?" I laugh.

He sets the breadstick down on the plate in front of him. "Are you nervous?" he asks as he leans back in his seat.

"A little bit," I say breathlessly. I shuffle in my seat, watching another couple get seated. "Besides Jake, I've never actually been on a date before. And I wouldn't necessarily call that one a success."

"Well, hey." Graham reaches for my hand and runs his thumb over my knuckles. He cocks his head to the left a bit and adds, "This can be whatever you want it to be."

I bite the inside of my cheek to keep from smiling even bigger than I already am.

Our waitress returns, takes our order and then takes off back to the kitchen. I busy myself with dishing out some salad as she walks away.

"How's your mom?" I ask as Graham starts to serve himself some of the salad.

"She's good," he says, setting his plate down and letting out a breath. "She's really excited I'm out with you."

"Oh?"

"She hasn't stopped talking about you since the festival."

I laugh. "No pressure, right?"

Graham chuckles now. "None." He picks up a forkful of salad. "I'm sure Raquel is just as excited as Mom."

I raise my eyebrows. "Why do you say that?"

"She's been on me to ask you out since you first moved here." He takes another careful bite.

Apparently, everyone wanted us together just like Judith wanted Charlie and Beth together.

"Well, hey," I say, my fork scraping my plate. "At least you finally did."

Graham opens his mouth to respond but is cut off when my phone rings.

"Sorry," I say as I pick it up. It's Beth; I know she wouldn't be calling unless it were important.

"Hey," I answer, slightly worried that something bad has happened.

"Hey," she says, "I'm sorry to disturb your date but Charlie just called. They arrested Jake."

"Really?" I ask. My eyes go wide and I look at Graham.

"James can't fix this one for him. I didn't want to wait to tell you. Figured you'd want to know."

"Yes, thank you."

"Anyways, I'll see you when you get home. I love you!"

"Love you, too." I disconnect the call and set my phone back down on the table.

"Is everything okay?" Graham asks.

I nod. "Yeah, that was Beth. She said Jake got arrested."

"Good," he says with a smile. "I had faith in Sheriff Gajewski."

"You can call him Charlie, ya know." I don't fight the grin that's blooming on my face.

"It's a respect thing for me." He takes another bite of salad.

I nod. Graham is such a sweetheart.

"How are he and Beth doing?" he asks. "Everyone at work is curious."

I stab my fork through some of the crunchy lettuce on my plate. "They're good," I say. "They're finally getting it right."

Graham reaches for my hand across the table and gently takes it in his. He rubs his thumbs over my knuckles.

"I think a few of us are finally getting it right."

After Regiano's, we head down to the pier for ice cream. It's busy tonight, as families try to squeeze in as much togetherness as they can before summer ends. It's nice being here with Graham. It feels like I've known him a lot longer than a single summer.

We both decide on ice cream cones — confetti cake for me and mint chocolate chip for Graham. I wouldn't have pegged him for a mint chocolate chip kind of guy but I'm still learning details about him. I'm excited to keep uncovering little treasures like this.

We slowly walk along the pier as we eat our ice cream, dodging families of all sizes and even some dogs. Graham stops and leans against the railing and I follow suit. The sun is setting, creating a beautiful, real-life watercolor painting before us. Streaks of pink and orange burst through bits of blue and it just might be one of the prettiest sunsets I've ever seen in my entire life.

We stay at the railing for a while after the sun sets, finishing our ice cream. The sky turns completely dark and the stars come out. I marvel at them. You can actually see the stars out here in Driftbay. I never really could back in Seattle.

Graham points out a shooting star and leans down to whisper in my ear.

"Close your eyes and make a wish," he murmurs.

I squeeze my eyes tight and know instantly what I want to wish for. I wish for more moments like this, moments that make me glad to be alive.

I open my eyes to see Graham staring at me in adoration. The warm breeze of salty air blows over my skin, giving me goosebumps.

"What?" I laugh.

"Just thinking," he murmurs.

"About what?"

"You know, I wanted to move away for so long," he says. "I thought that was what I wanted. But it turns out I was wrong all along. I think I was meant to stay in Driftbay, not only for my mom, but for a beautiful girl who loves to bake."

He leans forward and I feel my eyes flutter closed. His hand brushes my cheek and then he grasps the hair at the base of my neck. I tilt my head up and his lips are on mine — it's like time stops for a moment.

I swear I can hear fireworks going off in the distance, but it could just be my imagination. The butterflies in my stomach take flight and leave me breathless as we part. Graham looks at me like I'm the greatest thing he's ever seen.

"I have wanted to do that for so long," he says quietly. He smiles, his eyes sparkling. Everyone on the pier has faded away and I only see him.

"Really?" I ask.

"Was it not obvious?" he laughs.

"Maybe a little," I say as I shrug.

He takes my hand again and we begin to walk the length of the pier, now lit up with arcade lights from the various games and attractions, the scent of saltwater taffy making my mouth water. We head to the golf cart, continually bumping into each other as we walk. Like a true gentleman, he helps me step up into the golf cart before driving me home.

Graham cuts the engine after we pull into the driveway and we sit in silence for a few moments. I fiddle with the bouquet of daisies laying across my lap.

"What did you wish for?" he asks as we walk to the front door.

"I can't say or else it won't come true," I say, playfully hitting his shoulder. "Isn't that the rule?"

He smiles. "You've got me there."

Our fingers dance together, not wanting to finish their tango.

We stop in the doorway, our faces illuminated in the overhead security light and moonlight.

He leans in and softly presses a kiss to my cheek.

"I had a really nice time tonight, Graham," I whisper, looking up at him.

"I did, too. Should have asked you sooner."

A smile spreads across my face.

"See you tomorrow at work?" he asks.

"Yeah." I bite my lip as I nod.

"Good night, Thea."

"Good night, Graham." I watch as he heads back to the golf cart. He gives me a little wave as he takes off and disappears down the road out of sight.

I unlock the front door and step across the threshold into the house. I slowly shut the door behind me, waiting for the click of the doorknob to know it's truly shut. I flip the lock and deadbolt, then lean against the door, biting my lip. I smell my daisies again and replay the night's events in my head.

For a first date, it was pretty great.

I see the glow of a lamp spilling out of the living room, so I figure Beth is waiting up for me. I tiptoe around the corner and see her on the couch asleep, curled up with her book. Smiling, I gently take off her reading glasses and move her book to the coffee table before kissing the top of her head. I turn, my eyes landing on the urn in the middle of the mantle.

I wish my mother were here to see what Driftbay has given me, the people and the place that have grown so near and dear to my heart. I know she'd be happy that Beth has finally found happiness with Charlie and that I'm doing better. I'd like to think that she is smiling down on us from wherever she is.

I used to think of the accident as the derailing of my life, but now I'm starting to view it as redirection. How even in the midst of tragedy, something sweet can be found.

I smile to myself as I turn out the light, the room plunging into darkness.

# Epilogue

## Thea

Three Months Later

Today I'm baking something truly special — an engagement cake.

Charlie has requested Italian creme cake as a nod to their first date.

I've baked two layers of cake and have them set aside on the counter to cool. Penny has been tasked with keeping Beth out of the kitchen today, or at least until I leave. I wipe my hands on my apron as I glance at the clock across the kitchen — Charlie should be here soon to pick me up. I told Beth that I have an appointment with Amber, but really, we're getting ready for him to propose tonight. I feel bad lying to her, but the result will be so worth it.

Graham grins at me from across the kitchen. He has music blasting from a bluetooth speaker above his station on the grill. I can't help but laugh as he dances around the kitchen, singing along to the music as he cooks. He spins around from the grill to look at me intently, singing into his spatula the entire time. He reaches out his hand and I take it, grinning wildly as he spins me across the kitchen.

I grab a pastry box from underneath the counter and fold it together as I turn back to the cake. I'm pleased with it and I know Beth will be, too. I untie the apron from around my hips and toss it on the rack on the wall. Heading into the break room, I retrieve my phone and keys before walking back by Graham.

"Bye," he says as he plates a cheeseburger and fries.

"See you later," I reply before giving him a quick kiss on the lips.

The grill crackles in the background as we break apart. My stomach grumbles in protest as I breathe in the smell of the burgers, but I don't have time to stop and eat. Instead, I snatch a fry from the plate in his hand and pop it into my mouth.

"Good," I say, "but needs more salt."

Graham opens his mouth in protest but I dash to the counter to grab the cake box and shove my phone into my back pocket. I balance it on one hand as I quickly step out the back door, undetected by Beth. Penny is doing a good job of keeping her occupied.

Charlie is parked around back in his squad car. He watches me from behind his aviators as I walk down the steps of the diner, careful not to drop the box in my hands. The gravel crunches loudly underneath my feet as I hurry to the car. The cool breeze dries the sweat from my skin, and I can't help but wonder what winter will look like here in Driftbay in a few months.

Opening the back passenger door, I gently place the cake box on the floorboard and then climb into the passenger seat beside him.

"How's she doing?" he asks.

"Good, I think. I avoided her most of the day," I reply as I buckle my seatbelt. "Doesn't suspect a thing."

"Good, good."

I can tell Charlie is nervous by the way his hands are gripping the steering wheel. His knuckles are white.

He puts the car into reverse and we leave the diner, pulling out onto the main road to head back to the house. It's a quiet drive back.

One of the things I've been working on in therapy is my anxiety around vehicles. Some days still get the best of me, but I'm doing better than I have in a while. Amber and I have been working on the root cause of my fear and I've gotten better about being able to handle it.

I know Charlie is lost in his thoughts so I ask him, "Run me through it again?"

He lets out a nervous breath. "I'm cooking dinner for us all," he begins.

I nod. Charlie and Beth have never made me feel like a third wheel, always including me in their dinners at home. The three of us have become somewhat of a family unit, and I think Charlie understands that Beth and I are a package deal at this point.

"At sunset, I'm going to take Beth Ann down for a walk along the water and then...I'm going to propose."

"Are you nervous?" I ask, knowing that he most definitely is.

"More than I've ever been in my entire life," he admits.

He takes a left and pulls into the driveway. We sit there for a moment, neither of us moving.

"You know she's going to say yes," I say quietly.

"I hope so," he says. "This is the most important question of my life." He takes another deep breath in and leans against the headrest.

"Relax a little," I laugh, "It'll be fine." I undo my seatbelt and open the door to step out.

"Easy for you to say," he laughs as he gets out of the car, "you're not the one proposing."

I grab the cake box from the back of the car, kicking the door shut with my foot. I follow Charlie up the porch steps to the back door. He slides his key in and unlocks it, stepping aside and motioning for me to go in front of him. I head to the kitchen and set the box down on the counter before retrieving my ingredients for the icing.

Charlie's been preparing all morning; there're steaks marinating in the refrigerator and a bouquet of Beth's favorite flowers, zinnias and hydrangeas, on the table. I swear I can see a worn path on the floor from his pacing.

He follows me into the kitchen and rolls up the sleeves of his gray button-up shirt. Pointing at the flowers, he clears his throat and asks, "Do you think she'll like these?"

I turn from the cabinet, mixing bowl in hand. "I think she's going to love them," I say as I set it down on the counter.

The early October breeze is blowing through the slightly cracked kitchen window, curtains fluttering in the wind. Summer is well on its way out the door.

I grab the mixer from its permanent spot on the counter and dump my ingredients for the icing into the bowl. As I'm mixing them together, I catch myself thinking back on all that has happened in the short amount of time since I came to Drifbay.

I came here a lonely, brokenhearted girl, longing to feel whole again. I rebuilt myself in Driftbay. I found a job that I love, coworkers that became friends, a better relationship with my aunt, and a boyfriend. I found a great therapist, who's helped me along my walk with grief.

I've come to realize that it's true what people say about your loved ones always being with you after they die. I see pieces of my mom everywhere. She's there in the way that Penny expresses herself, in Graham's fierce loyalty and love, and in Raquel's stormy attitude. Together, they make me feel less alone and help keep her flame alive.

Once I'm satisfied with the consistency of my icing, I grab a display platter and a knife. I unbox the cake layers and plate it, getting to work on icing it. I hum while I work, inhaling the sweet smell of vanilla. I fill a piping bag with more icing and make some simple swirls across the top of the cake. I become lost in my confectionary world while Charlie paces behind me.

"It's going to be fine," I say as I finish piping and admire my handiwork. "She's going to say yes and you'll get your happily ever after." I pick up the plate and put the cake in the fridge. "You have nothing to worry about." I transfer my dishes to the sink and turn the water on, letting it run over my hands as it heats up.

"I just want to make her happy," I hear him mutter.

"You do. She wouldn't have stuck around this long if you didn't. Now, go watch TV or something to get your mind off of it, or you'll drive yourself mad." I turn around and shoo him away from the kitchen. "Beth won't be home for another couple of hours."

I finish washing the dishes before retreating to my room. I want to stay out of Charlie's way. He's already nervous enough without me hovering. I shut my bedroom door and flop down on my bed before pulling out my phone. I stare at the black screen and decide to call Ireland. We haven't talked much this summer. I dial her number and listen to the ringing tone while I wait for her to pick up. She answers on the second ring.

"Well, hey there, stranger!" she exclaims. I can hear Tucker barking in the background.

"Hi," I say, smiling at the familiarity. It's like no time has passed between us.

"How are you?" she asks. "We haven't talked in forever."

"I know and I'm sorry about that," I say. Truly, I am. "But I'm good," I add, "how are things back in Seattle?"

I stare across my room and my eyes settle on the framed photo of Beth, Mom, and me, the one placed in here to welcome me. The heart-shaped seashell Graham found for me sits against it and I can't help but smile.

"Well," Ireland starts, "I'm moving."

"What? No way!" I exclaim.

"Yep." I can sense her nodding through the phone. "You've inspired me to get out of here."

"Where are you going?"

"I think I'm going to travel for a bit. See where the wind takes me."

She's always been somewhat of a free spirit.

"Tell me about your summer," she adds. "I want to hear all about it."

So I tell her. I tell her about Jake, about meeting my new friends Raquel and Penny. I tell her about Beth and Charlie, how I almost got in legal trouble for underage drinking, how I ended up in the hospital, and about my therapist. The most exciting part was telling her that my heart now belongs to a sandy-haired, blue eyed boy named Graham. How he showed up like a knight on his white golf cart to sweep me off my feet.

We end up talking for a few hours before we hang up.

Charlie is back in the kitchen later that evening, searing steaks when we hear Beth come home. I duck my head out into the hallway and watch as she shrugs off her jacket and hangs it on a hook by the door.

"Hi," she says, smiling as she sees me. She runs a hand through her hair, exhaustion clear in the slump of her shoulders.

"Hi!" I reply, a little too peppy. She doesn't seem to notice.

I sit down at the table as Beth walks down the hallway and into the kitchen, noticing the flowers on the table first. She lifts them to her nose, closing her eyes as she inhales deeply, savoring the sweet fragrance.

"These are beautiful," she says as she sets them back down on the table.

Charlie turns from the stove and smiles. I look at him with a smirk on my face, as if to say, *I told you so.*

"Hi," he says.

She walks over to him and kisses his cheek. "Hi," she repeats. "What's for dinner?" she asks, glancing over his shoulder at what's cooking in the pan.

"Steaks seared in garlic butter, diced potatoes, and caesar salad."

"A feast," she says. "Maybe *you* should come work at the diner," she jokes.

Charlie reaches for his phone and changes the music playing through the Bluetooth speaker to some upbeat, jazzy pop song as Beth pulls her sleeves up.

"What can I do to help?"

"Not a thing," he says, with a grin and adds, "tonight is all about you."

"All about me? What did I do to deserve this?" Beth asks.

Charlie responds with a kiss and pulls out a chair for her. "Now, sit down. You've had a long day at work."

I jump up from the table and open the fridge, retrieving the salad kit. I busy myself with fixing the salad while Beth sits down.

"How was the rest of your day?" Charlie asks as he adjusts the heat on the stove.

"We were slammed all day. I don't think I sat down once. My feet hurt so bad," she says.

"Hmm, sounds like a foot rub is in order."

"Dinner and a foot rub? Okay, what is going on here?" Beth asks with a laugh, her gaze darting between us.

I pour the dressing into the bowl in front of me, along with the cheese and croutons, and then start searching for a pair of tongs. I can't look at her. She can read my face like an open book and I know if I make eye contact, somehow she will *know*.

I find the tongs and toss the salad before getting the cake out of the fridge.

"Italian creme cake?" Beth asks, jumping up out of the chair as she sees it.

Her eyes twinkle as she comes over to the counter. Charlie smiles as he watches her, a look of pure love on his face.

I take the plastic wrap off the cake and Beth swipes her finger through some of the icing.

"Oh, my God," she mutters as she licks her finger. "Thea, you've outdone yourself."

"Thanks," I say, with a grin. Charlie pulls a ring box from his pocket and gets down on one knee behind her.

"Beth Ann," he says. It's barely audible but Beth turns around, slowly removing her finger from her mouth. She wipes it on her jeans as Charlie takes her left hand in his.

Beth freezes.

"You know, I had this big romantic gesture planned," he says. "I was going to take you down to the beach at sunset, but I can't wait a minute longer. Beth Ann, I want you to be my wife."

Beth blinks rapidly, a blush rising to her cheeks.

"I've been late for a lot of things in my life," Charlie continues, "but my biggest regret has been that I waited so long to tell you how I really feel. It's you, it's always been you. I've loved you for three decades now; I want them all. So, will you do me the honor of wearing my ring and becoming my wife?"

He opens the ring box, revealing the emerald cut ring he'd had custom-made for her.

"Charlie," she says in a breathy voice, "I don't know what to say."

"Say yes," he pleads as he looks up at her.

I hold my breath as I await her answer. Seconds tick by, the only sound in the kitchen is the steaks sizzling.

"Yes," she says. It comes out a whisper but Charlie jumps to his feet as if she had screamed it.

"Yes! Yes, absolutely!"

They crash into each other, hugging and laughing and kissing. I let out a breath I didn't realize I'd been holding. They part and he takes the ring out of the box and slides it onto her finger.

It's kind of poetic that Charlie chose to propose in the kitchen, at least for us. It's where we've worked through our feelings, both big and small. Love, loss, and every feeling in between have taken seats at the table. We've baked through every emotion under the sun within these walls, so it's only fitting that the best one of all be whipped up in a moment of surprise.

"Congratulations," I say and they welcome me into their embrace. The three of us stand there in the kitchen, hugging like the newfound family that we are.

After a delicious celebratory dinner, I retreat to my room. I grab my journal and a towel and head down to the beach. Amber recommended journaling as a way to help process my grief, so each night at sunset I have a journaling session by the ocean.

There're a few groups of people on the beach this evening, though it's nothing compared to how busy it was over the summer. Some are playing volleyball, some still relax in their chairs. A flock of seagulls chirp and fly overhead. I trudge through the soft white sand down toward the water's edge, my towel slung over my shoulder.

I approach my usual vicinity just out of reach of the waves and stop, reaching for my towel. I shake it out and lay it down on the sand and then kick my sandals off before sitting down in the middle of the towel, the worn fabric comforting on my skin.

I open my journal up to today's date and taking a deep breath, uncap the pen. There's music in the distance barely audible over the crashing of waves. It's faint but I'd recognize it anywhere. Dreams by Fleetwood Mac — Mom's favorite song. I begin writing and once I start, I can't stop. I write about Beth and Charlie's engagement, and how he is becoming the closest thing I've ever had to a father figure. As silly as it sounds, I write about the relief I feel that the engagement cake turned out so wonderfully.

I want Ireland to come out here to visit, to see the town that has stolen my heart. I write about Graham, and wonder if he's becoming my own Charlie — if we'll have a love story that spans decades. He was the golden thread that tied my broken edges back together.

I write about how much I miss my mom and wish she were here to see how I've grown and how happy Beth is with Charlie. I write about wanting to open my own bakery here some day and how my goals are so vastly different than they were a year ago. How I now have purpose and drive.

But mostly, what I write about is...following my heart. I think that's the biggest lesson I've learned with my mother's passing. Life is short and tomorrow isn't promised. Happiness can be created in the saddest of circumstances, whether it be found in a relationship or recipe.

Besides, a wise old woman once told me that the heart wants what the heart wants.

# Acknowledgements

They say writing is a solitary profession. I would have to disagree. I have so many wonderful people in my life that helped me along this journey and would be remiss if I didn't send a special thanks to them.

God - from whom all blessings flow. I am overjoyed that this story was placed on my heart and I was given the tools to tell it.

Mom - for always encouraging my love of reading and writing, from a very young age (and buying many a laptop when I'd wear one out). You've always been in my corner and my loudest cheerleader and I couldn't have done this without your support.

My best friend, Peyton - the yin to my yang, the Glinda to my Elphie. Your unwavering friendship has been a constant in my life and I don't know what I would do without it. I hope I made you proud. "Because I knew you, I have been changed for good."

M - although I didn't know what to call it at the time, thank you for being my original beta reader all those years ago as well as being a great source of inspiration. Your support has meant more than you'll ever know.

Mrs. G - my junior high English/Language Arts teacher for encouraging me to keep writing. You spent countless hours cheering me on, helping me edit, spending your personal time at writing award banquets, and so much more. I wouldn't be where I am today without your love and guidance.

Penny - for being my #1 hype-woman and loving these characters so authentically that it kept me going even on my worst day.

Charlotte - my editor, friend, and co-worker, for cheering me on, pushing me to the best of my abilities, and lending your personal time and creative abilities to help me achieve my dream. I am forever in your debt.

Delaney - for your beautiful artwork as well as your even more beautiful friendship. I am so thankful to know you and love you.

My friends - Laura, Maggie, Rianne, Raquel, Kendra, Taylor, Emma, Jenny, Madison, Taylor F, and so many more - you each are special to me in your own way. I'm grateful for each and every one of you and the role you played in bringing this story to life.

My beta readers - thank you for being so enthusiastic and helping shape this story.

Lastly, to all of the incredible women I know that inspired this book - whether they know it or not. If a character was named after you or your essence sparked the creative flame, thank you. These characters are the combination of women I admire and I am so lucky to have such strong, badass influences in my life.

# About the Author

Ellis Darnell is a Midwest native who has enjoyed reading and writing from a very young age. In her spare time, she can be found collecting vinyl records, hanging out with her two cats, and traveling. She is also heavily involved in her local theatre scene, having been a stage manager for the last thirteen years. You can find her online at @authorellisdarnell.

www.ingramcontent.com/pod-product-compliance
Lightning Source LLC
LaVergne TN
LVHW041154150826
845673LV00001B/155

* 9 7 9 8 9 9 5 2 1 0 2 0 7 *